Wishbone barked as loud...
"Sound the ala...
clubhouse!" h...

Joe looked down at the pools of water forming on the floor. "Oh, no, the creek's probably overflowing, and we're in a low-lying area!" Joe ran to the front door and tugged, but nothing happened. "It won't open!" he cried.

Next, Sam went to the front door and pulled on it, but it still didn't budge. "I can't open it!" she shouted. She raised her feet one at a time, trying to prevent her sneakers from getting soaked. "And the water's getting higher!

"Let's try the windows," Sam said. "They're not big enough for us to crawl through, but Wishbone can. Then he can go for help!"

Joe raced over to one of the windows and tried to open it. But it wouldn't move. "It's stuck!" Joe shouted.

WISHBONE Mysteries

THE HAUNTED CLUBHOUSE

by Caroline Leavitt

WISHBONE™ created by Rick Duffield

Big Red Chair Books™, *A Division of **Lyrick Publishing**™*

This book is a work of fiction. The characters, incidents, and dialogues are products of the author's imagination and are not to be construed as real. Any resemblance to actual events or persons, living or dead, is entirely coincidental.

 Big Red Chair Books™, *A Division of Lyrick Publishing*™
300 E. Bethany Drive, Allen, Texas 75002

©1997 Big Feats! Entertainment

Edited by Kevin Ryan

Copy edited by Jonathon Brodman

Cover concept and design Lyle Miller

Interior illustrations by Jane McCreary

Wishbone photograph by Carol Kaelson

Library of Congress Catalog Card Number: 97-73281

ISBN: 1-57064-280-X

First printing: November 1997

10 9 8 7 6 5 4 3 2 1

Printed in the United States of America

For my mother, Helen Leavitt,
who always sees the beauty
and mystery in life

FROM THE BIG RED CHAIR . . .

Oh . . . hi! Wishbone here. You caught me right in the middle of some of my favorite things—books. Let me welcome you to my brand-new book series, WISHBONE MYSTERIES. In each story, I help my human friends solve a puzzling mystery. In *THE HAUNTED CLUBHOUSE*, I work alongside my best friend, Joe, to figure out what's causing the mysterious, strange, and scary goings-on in a neighborhood clubhouse.

This story takes place early in the school year, just before the events that you'll see in the second season of my WISHBONE television show. In this story, Joe is fourteen and just starting the eighth grade. Just like me, he's always ready for adventure.

You're in for a real treat, so pull up a chair and a snack and sink your teeth into *THE HAUNTED CLUBHOUSE*!

Chapter One

Wishbone ran through the neighborhood on his way home. It was Sunday evening at five, and the weather was perfect. The breeze ruffled Wishbone's fur almost as pleasantly as if someone were petting him gently, just the way he liked. *Somebody like Joe,* Wishbone thought. Then he ran a little faster. The clouds floating overhead in the sky were pure white and shaped deliciously like bones. Gazing up at them, Wishbone wanted to leap high up into the air to try to catch a bite. It was late summer weather, that special time of year when everyone felt restless and *anything* could happen . . . and anything was about to.

"Paws going into second gear!" Wishbone cried as he speeded up. "I have to get home to Joe. Then we're both going to Jackson Park! That's where the raffle drawing will take place! I sure hope Joe wins."

Wishbone leaped over a mud puddle.

"I'll catch you later!" he called to the puddle.

He ran past Wanda's yard.

"Don't take it personally that I'm not stopping for

a friendly dig," Wishbone said. He stepped on a squeak toy he had left near Wanda's yard. It gave a loud *squawk!* "We'll continue our conversation later," Wishbone told the toy. "Right now I'm in too much of a hurry! I don't want to be even a minute late for the drawing."

Wishbone arrived at his house just in time to see Joe, crouched down on the front lawn, staring at his bike. Joe was Wishbone's best friend. Joe's bike was lying on its side in the grass. Beside it was the bicycle pump Joe had brought outside from the garage.

Joe doesn't look too happy, Wishbone thought. *I wonder what's wrong.* He barked a greeting. "Hey, Joe, I'm here! Happiness can't be far behind."

Joe looked up. "Hi, Wishbone," Joe said. He pressed his hands along one of the bike's tires. "How could I have a problem with my bike again? Every time I need my bike so I can be somewhere important, this happens."

"It's not *every* time, Joe," Wishbone said. "It was just *one* other time that we were knocked flat. I always try to block that out from my memory, because Bruno the Doberman was involved."

Joe checked his watch and sighed. Wishbone noticed Joe had that worried look he sometimes got. When that happened even Wishbone himself couldn't charm Joe out of his mood. Joe got up and bounded into the house. Wishbone followed at his heels. He knew that whether Joe realized it or not, Joe needed him close at hand during times like this.

Inside, Ellen Talbot, Joe's mother and the Keeper of All Tasty Snacks, was sitting in the big red chair by the window, writing a letter. Her hair was the same deep brown shade as Joe's. She was wearing a pair of shoes that were Wishbone's favorite—soft brown leather loafers that made Wishbone's teeth ache to chew on them.

"Don't worry, Ellen, I'm taking good care of Joe," Wishbone said.

"My tire needs air, and my pump doesn't work. Didn't Dad keep an old bicycle pump up in the attic? I just want to hurry and fix it and get to the raffle drawing," Joe said.

Ah, so that's why Joe is so glum, Wishbone thought. He was as excited as Joe was about the raffle, but there was no need to worry about being late for the drawing. Wishbone was sure they'd win. He felt it in his bones, which was a feeling dogs always relied on.

"I know, honey," Ellen said, standing up. "It's really exciting, isn't it? I think everyone I know bought a raffle ticket."

"It's all I can think about," Joe said. "I can't sit still. That's why I want to hurry and fix the bike and get to Jackson Park early."

Ellen put her pen down. "I'm pretty sure there's a pump in the attic. But don't ask me where. If you can't find it, my offer to drive you over to the park still stands, if you don't mind going a little later."

"That would be great," Joe said.

"Be careful when you go up into the attic," Ellen said. "I should follow the Oakdale Historical Society's example of tidying up old landmarks and do our own cleanup."

"Ellen, why don't you clean up the way I do?"

Wishbone said. "Bury everything in the backyard or stash it under the couch. There's still plenty of room in both spots."

Ellen stretched. "I keep meaning to get up there and straighten things up, but something else always comes up. Who knows what you'll find?"

"Yeah! There could be snacks, or balls or chew toys!" Wishbone said.

Joe made his way up the stairs to the attic. Wishbone was close behind him, his nails clicking on the wooden steps. Joe didn't go up into the attic very often. Most of the things up there were his mom's. That was where she stored old clothing, furniture she didn't want to throw away, and odds and ends. Anything Joe really wanted or needed, he kept in his room, right where he could see it.

At the top of the staircase, Joe opened the door to the attic and switched on the light. The attic was small, with wood floors and one long sloping wall. Boxes were strewn about everywhere. An old green bicycle leaned against one wall. A chest of drawers was pushed up against another wall, alongside an old steamer trunk.

"Will you look at this?" Joe said.

He bent down and picked up one of the boxes. Its lid came open, and an old red-and-white cowboy outfit fell out. Joe picked it up. He held it against his chest.

"I wore this when I was five years old!" he said. He looked affectionately at it. "That's people years, not dog years," he said to Wishbone.

Wishbone cocked his head, making Joe grin. Joe never stopped being surprised by Wishbone. He loved the fact that no matter what he said, Wishbone always seemed to understand him completely. Sometimes he even thought Wishbone was part human.

Wishbone nosed around, sneezing from the dust. Suddenly the canine with super-sharp eyesight spotted something under a pile of old magazines, and he began to dig enthusiastically. His tail wagged excitedly, keeping a kind of beat.

"Are you finding buried treasure, Wishbone?" Joe asked.

Wishbone tugged out an old blue leash.

Joe picked it up. "That was yours when you were just a puppy," he said. "Look how worn it is. We sure took a lot of walks with this, didn't we?"

Wishbone barked, and Joe handed him the leash. Instantly, Wishbone buried it under some boxes.

"Saving it for later?" Joe asked.

Wishbone let out another bark, apparently meaning "yes."

"Now, where's that bicycle pump?" Joe said. He looked over in one corner. There was an old coat rack. Hanging on it was one of Ellen's old hats, with an ornamental flower attached to it. Joe picked it up, glanced at it, and then quickly set it back on the rack. "There's something that belongs to everyone up here," Joe said.

He moved farther into the attic. His hand brushed along a wall, touching something small and soft and quick-moving. He squinted at it in the dim light. It was a small gray spider scuttling up the wall. Surprised, Joe backed up quickly, then stumbled forward, right into a cardboard wardrobe, and he knocked it over. Joe tripped, then fell on his hands and knees.

"Ow!" He winced. Wishbone ran over to Joe, cocking his head in concern. "I'm fine, Wishbone," Joe said. He got up off the floor and was about to set the wardrobe upright again, when he noticed a big cardboard box sitting behind it. He wondered what might be in there. Joe tugged the box out into the center of the attic.

Wishbone suddenly perked up. He sniffed furiously around the sides of the box. His tail wagged feverishly, and he began to bark louder and louder.

"What is it?" Joe asked. "Is that a box of your chew toys or something?"

Joe peered closely at the box from where he stood. It was all taped up, and there was a fine layer of dust on top of it. Joe sneezed. Then he brushed off some of the dust. He bent down to get a closer view of the box. Wishbone put his paws up on one of the top flaps and sniffed. The more he sniffed, the more his tail wagged.

"Calm down," Joe said. "You can have first dibs on whatever is in there, okay? Especially if it's chew toys." He rubbed Wishbone's fur behind his neck, right where he knew Wishbone liked to be stroked. "And if there are no chew toys in there, I'll buy you one tomorrow."

There was writing on the box.

"Mom labels everything," Joe said. "It's probably just some old dishes." Wishbone nudged at Joe with his nose. "Okay, okay, don't be so impatient. I'm going to open it," Joe said.

Joe brushed more of the dust away with his

hands. He bent over and blew at the remaining dust. Then, suddenly, he saw what was written there: STEVE TALBOT. His father's name. A chill ran down Joe's spine. Joe's father, Steve, had been a basketball coach at Oakdale College. He had died of a rare blood disorder eight years ago, when Joe was only six years old. Joe couldn't recall too much about his father, but he remembered that his dad had been tall and thin. He also had had the same dark hair Joe did, and the same brown eyes. Sometimes people even told Joe that he looked like his dad had. Joe was always thrilled to hear that.

At times, Joe enjoyed sitting and reminiscing about special moments he had shared with his father: his dad teaching him how to shoot hoops on summer

nights; his dad taking him fishing and carrying him around on his shoulders, and taking him to the tire swing in the park. Joe also was still able to recall how he had pulled at a wishbone when he was little, wishing for a puppy. His dad had then surprised him with Wishbone.

Joe began to peel the tape off the box. His heart raced at the thought of what he might find inside. He had trouble making his hands work properly. It seemed to take forever to pull off all the old, sticky tape. Wishbone stood up on his hind legs, leaning against the box with his front paws. He wagged his tail at full speed.

"Did you know this box was my dad's, Wishbone?" Joe asked. "Is that why you're so excited?"

After removing the last bits of tape, Joe opened the top flap. He tried to imagine what might be inside his father's box. Basketball shoes, maybe. Or perhaps it was photographs of the teams he coached. Maybe newspaper clippings about the games he had won. Joe pulled the final flap open. To his surprise, the box was filled with books. It looked as if there were at least fifty of them, maybe more, closely packed in together.

Joe began to pull out books from the box and look at them. There were all kinds of books by all sorts of writers, some he had never heard of. There was a collection of stories by the mystery writer Edgar Allan Poe, whose name Joe knew from school. A few titles were written by somebody named Raymond Chandler. There was a book by Mark Twain called *Tom Sawyer, Detective*. At the bottom of the box was a slim red volume with a picture of ten small Indians on the cover.

14

"Agatha Christie," Joe read out loud. *"Ten Little Indians.* I wonder what kind of book this is."

Wishbone rubbed his nose against Joe, as if encouraging him to continue. Joe turned the book over.

"'Ten people are invited to an island by a mysterious host,'" Joe said, reading the cover copy out loud. "'One by one they reveal their secrets. And one by one they disappear. But why?'" He looked up from the book for a moment. "Hey, that sounds like a great story. Right, Wishbone?"

Wishbone answered with a short bark.

Joe opened up the book. On the inside cover was some handwriting. Joe bent forward and began to read. "'This book belongs to Steve Talbot,'" he said. He felt another chill run down his spine. Joe was looking at his father's writing! The letters were strongly made, as if his dad had pressed down hard when he wrote. The *t*'s were crossed with a flourish. Joe traced the letters with his finger. The first *T* in "Talbot" was twice as big as the rest of the letters in the word. It was his name, but in his father's handwriting, it suddenly seemed brand-new and kind of mysterious. Joe liked the way it looked. He thought he'd start writing his last name the same way his father had. He began to practice, drawing the letters in the air with a finger.

Joe tried to imagine his father writing in the book. Had he sat in the big red chair downstairs to write his name in it? Had he read this volume all in one sitting, or had he taken his time, reading a chapter a night? Joe sat down and was silent. He stared at the book, thumbing through the pages. As he turned each page, he imagined his father doing the same.

Joe closed the book thoughtfully. He stood up and put it back in the box. As he looked up, he saw something in one corner. He squinted. Why, it was his dad's old bicycle pump, hidden in plain sight! Joe shook his head in amusement at himself, and he walked over to it. He bent down and scooped up the pump, tucking it under one arm. Then he put the pump on top of the box and carried them both away from the dimness of the attic.

"Come on, Wishbone," Joe said. "Let's go downstairs. I can't wait to show these books to Mom."

Wishbone followed Joe downstairs as closely as he could. Now that he recognized the special scent of Steve Talbot's books, he couldn't get enough of them. Every sniff reminded him of how Joe's father had petted him on the head or taken him and Joe for long walks. He knew how important the books were to Joe by the careful way in which Joe carried them.

Wishbone got back to Ellen first. "Ellen, look what we have!" Wishbone called. Wishbone watched as Joe came into the room and set down the box of books in front of Ellen.

"I see you found the pump," Ellen said. "But what's in that box?"

"Wait until you see!" Joe said, showing her the box. Wishbone heard the excitement in Joe's voice.

Ellen's face lit up when she looked inside the box of books. "Oh, my, this is wonderful. These are your father's favorite mystery stories," Ellen said. "I packed them away for safekeeping and then forgot about them." She picked one up and held it gently. "You know, your father loved nothing more than a good mystery. He sometimes used to drive me crazy trying to figure out the solution before the book ended." She smiled affectionately.

Joe held up the book by Agatha Christie. "I want to read this one."

Wishbone stood on his hind legs and put his paws up on the box. "Agatha Christie!" Wishbone said. "Why, she's one of the greatest mystery writers of all time—and a personal favorite of mine. She was a best-selling author who wrote almost one hundred mysteries. She was even honored by the queen of England and was made a Dame of the British Empire!"

A dame, in case you were wondering, is a female knight. England shows its appreciation for talented people by "knighting" them, or honoring them, with special names. A knighted woman is called "dame." A knighted man is called "sir." It's sort of like naming a dog "Best of Show"! Many of Agatha Christie's mystery books have been made into movies, too. I've only seen them when they play on television, though, because for some odd reason, movie theaters don't allow dogs. I don't understand that at all. We like popcorn as much as the next person.

"I wish I knew more about this writer," Joe said.

"Joe, Joe . . ." Wishbone sighed. "I just *told* you something about Agatha Christie! Why doesn't anybody ever listen to the dog?"

"You'll learn as you read," Ellen said. "Or you can go to the library and do some research."

Joe nodded. "So, was Dad able to figure out the mysteries?" Joe asked.

Ellen smiled again. "Sometimes," she said. "But those were the books he donated to the library. He usually kept the mysteries that surprised him. Those were the books he really loved."

"Well, I love a good mystery, too," Wishbone declared. "Like, why can't lunch be served three times a day instead of just once?"

"I wonder if I could figure out this mystery," Joe said, leafing through the pages.

Ellen looked at the book. "*Ten Little Indians.* That's a good one," she said.

"One of my favorites," said Wishbone.

"I'm going to read all of these books," Joe said.

Wishbone barked. "Devour every word, Joe!" he said.

Ellen grew thoughtful. "I'm glad you found your dad's books, Joe. And I'm thrilled that you're going to read them." She stood up, glancing at her watch. "It's almost time for the raffle drawing."

Joe nodded. "I just have to pump some air into my weak tire."

"I'll meet you guys at the park," Ellen said affectionately. "I have some chores I need to finish up. I'm going to drive over there a bit later."

Joe set off to go outside and pump up his bike tire. Wishbone trotted after him. The bicycle pump was old, but it still worked. In almost no time at all, Joe had pumped the problem tire full of air. Joe gave it a squeeze, making sure it felt sturdy. Then he crouched down and put his ear next to the tire to see if he could hear the slow hiss of air that meant there was a leak. Wishbone's ears perked up as Joe listened to the tire. No sound.

Satisfied, Joe put the pump in the garage. He came back out and got on his bike. "Maybe I'll end up with two prizes today—the raffle's grand prize, plus my father's books! I'm going to start reading as soon as we get home," Joe said.

"Two prizes! It all makes me wish that I had two tails to wag instead of just one," said Wishbone. "I sure hope you win, Joe!" He looked ahead down the street. "Now, let's go!"

Chapter Two

Wishbone couldn't contain his excitement. His steps bounced, his tail wagged, and his ears perked forward. He trotted beside Joe's bike as Joe pedaled right into Jackson Park. By the time they got to the middle of the park, where the drawing was going to be held, Wishbone was panting with anticipation.

Many of Wishbone's favorite people had already gathered there: Samantha, David, Mr. Pruitt, and Mr. Barnes. And Wanda Gilmore was there, too. They were all admiring the grand prize—an antique clubhouse! For the entire week leading up to the raffle drawing, the clubhouse was all anyone in Oakdale could talk about. It had been built way back in the early 1930s, and was made of soft pine. Wishbone thought the clubhouse was big, very big. It was taller than Joe, at least a few feet taller. And it was longer than it was tall. To Wishbone, the clubhouse looked like a big rectangle with a roof that sloped down from the front to the back. The wood had a beautiful pattern of whorls and circles in it, and it had turned a light gray—because of its age, Wishbone guessed.

Wishbone had heard Joe tell Ellen story after story about the clubhouse. For years, the clubhouse had sat unused in the Oakdale Historical Society's storage center. But this year, the historical society needed to raise money to continue its work, and raffling off the beautiful antique clubhouse would bring in much-needed funds. The society had set the clubhouse down in Jackson Park, right by some of Wishbone's favorite oak trees. Wanda, an important member of the society, had arranged for a flatbed truck to transport the clubhouse to the winner's home that very evening.

Just about everyone in Oakdale had bought a ticket. Wishbone looked over at the clubhouse. It was set in a low-lying area, near the Oakdale Creek, so the gurgling of the water could be heard. It was a pleasant sound, like a friendly voice telling Wishbone what a good dog he was.

People were excitedly going in and out of the clubhouse. On one side of the clubhouse, a big red flatbed truck was parked. There was a forklift strapped to the back, and the clubhouse sat on small cinder blocks, ready to be loaded onto the truck.

"Boy, that would be something to chase," Wishbone mused, looking at the truck. "Now, that's what I call a challenge."

On the other side of the clubhouse was something equally exciting to Wishbone—a long table filled with refreshments. There were jelly doughnuts, two yellow cakes, a big platter of blueberry muffins, and pitchers filled with punch.

21

"Come on, Wishbone. Let's go talk to Sam and David. I want to go inside the clubhouse and look it over before the drawing," Joe said.

"Good idea. I want to sniff around inside," Wishbone said. He gave the muffins one last look. "Don't go away, we'll be right back," he promised the refreshments.

Joe felt really nervous. He kept switching his balance from one leg to the other. He folded his arms and then unfolded them. He put his hands in his pockets and then took them out again. He looked at the outside of the clubhouse and realized how much he wanted it.

Joe wanted to stand inside the cool, old structure and imagine what it might feel like to own such a great place. Joe walked toward his friends Samantha and David, who were standing just outside the clubhouse.

"Hi, Joe. Hi, Wishbone," Sam said, stooping to scratch Wishbone behind his ears. Wishbone wagged his whole body happily. "I'm so nervous," Sam said. "I hope one of us wins."

"Don't you like the idea of having a place that would be ours alone? We could camp out and play cards and just hang out in there," Joe said. He ran his hands along the outside walls of the clubhouse.

"Let's go inside and check it out," David said.

Just then, Mr. Barnes and Mr. Pruitt came out of the clubhouse. Both men were smiling. "This will make a great playhouse for Emily and her friends," Mr. Barnes said to Mr. Pruitt.

Mr. Pruitt nodded and looked at the clubhouse. "It seems to be a very comfortable kind of place. If I win, I'm going to use it as a writing studio." He looked over at Wanda, who was setting a large fishbowl filled with the raffle tickets on a big table.

Damont Jones walked by. He was an athletic boy, Joe's age. Joe always tried his best to get along with everyone, but sometimes it was hard to like Damont. Damont always pushed himself into competition with Joe for something. Damont had to be the best basketball player, the best soccer player, the best everything.

Damont pushed his baseball cap back on his head. He nodded at Joe. "If I win, I'm going to charge people admission to see the clubhouse. And I'm going to charge double if they want to go inside. I'll make a bundle," he said.

Samantha rolled her eyes.

"And no dogs allowed," Damont said to Wishbone, who stood closer to Joe.

"What about you, Joe? What would you do if you won?" Mr. Pruitt asked.

"I'd use it as a clubhouse for me and my friends," Joe said.

Mr. Pruitt blinked and then laughed. "What a great idea," said Mr. Pruitt. "A clubhouse used as a — well—a clubhouse!" He held out his hand for Joe to shake. "Good luck, Joe."

"Good luck to you, too," Joe said.

The kids watched Mr. Pruitt and Mr. Barnes walk away. In the distance, Joe saw his mother park her car.

Then she walked toward Wanda, who was waving gaily to her.

"Who knows who will win?" Sam said. "And who knows if whoever wins will want anyone else visiting their treasured prize? Even for admission fees, like Damont wants to do."

"So this might be the last time we get to go inside and check it out," David said.

"The last time?" Joe asked. "But—but this is going to be my very first time! And if it's also my last, that would be terrible."

Wishbone tumbled beside Joe and then looked up at him anxiously. Joe patted Wishbone's head, but he couldn't keep his eyes off the clubhouse.

"Let's go inside right now," Joe said. "Come on, Wishbone."

The inside of the clubhouse was eight feet high, perfect to stand up in, but not so high that anyone would feel lost inside it. The floor was made of the same pine as the walls. The door swung open and shut easily, so Wishbone could go in and out as he pleased.

Joe pointed to a corner by a window. "I could put a chair there for reading," he said. Then he pointed to a space by the door. "And we could have a table over there for snacks."

Wishbone trotted over to another window, barking for Joe to notice him.

David ran his hand along the walls. "And look at the patterns in the wood!" David exclaimed. "That one looks like a horse!"

Sam stared at the wall that David was describing. Then she pointed to the far wall. "That one, with the

dark swirl, looks like a face staring right at us," Sam said. "It's kind of creepy."

"Where?" Joe said.

Sam pointed again to the far wall, but all Joe could see was the gray wood.

"I don't see any dark swirl," David said.

"It's right there," Sam said impatiently. She looked over at the far wall again and seemed startled. There was only a smooth expanse of gray wood. There was no dark swirl. "I saw it right there a second ago," she insisted. "But now it's gone."

Just then, two more people came inside to examine the interior of the clubhouse. There was a young, wiry boy Joe's age. He had the same bright red hair as the little girl with him, and the two kids both had the same brilliant blue eyes. Joe recognized the boy. He was Bobby Maxwell, a new student at school. He wasn't in any of Joe's classes. However, Joe had noticed him walking in the halls because he was so full of energy, and because he always seemed to be carrying some intriguing item. Earlier that day, Joe had seen him with a small telescope. The day before, Bobby had been carrying a globe the size of a large basketball.

At the moment, Bobby was carrying a pair of binoculars. His eyes danced and sparkled, and he kept moving around inside the clubhouse. He touched the walls. He bent and touched the floor. He looked out of one of the clubhouse windows with his binoculars. He looked around with such a sense of delighted amazement that Joe began to feel thrilled, too.

The girl, Joe thought, must be Bobby's sister. But she seemed different to Joe than Bobby did. She was as still as Bobby was full of motion. She stood in one place beside Bobby, her hands deep in her pockets. The only thing similar about the two of them besides their hair and eyes was that they both had freckles like tiny copper pennies. If anyone took the time to count them, Joe thought, they'd probably add up to enough pennies to buy a dog toy for Wishbone.

Bobby raced over to another one of the windows. The girl trailed him like a shadow. He touched a pane of glass. She stood on tiptoes and touched the glass, too. Bobby turned to her and sighed. "You don't have to follow me so closely," he said.

"I'm not. I was coming here on my own," she protested. She noticed Wishbone and bent to pet him. "What a beautiful dog," she said softly. Wishbone licked her hand.

Joe walked over to Bobby and the girl. "You're Bobby Maxwell, the new kid," he said. Then Joe looked from Bobby to the little girl. She seemed really shy to

Joe. She wouldn't look him in the eye, but she kept watching Wishbone.

"This is my sister, Henrietta," Bobby said. "She's only nine."

"Nine's a great age," Joe said encouragingly, but Henrietta still wouldn't meet his gaze.

David walked over and grinned at Bobby. "I've already met Bobby," David said. "He knows everything about space. His father's an astronomer at the college. Bobby's even got a telescope set up in his backyard that he said we could come and look at."

Bobby's face lit up at the mention of the telescope. "Of course you can. I can show you the moon! Wait until you see how brilliant the stars look! It's incredible." Bobby handed Joe his binoculars. "Take a look out the window!" Bobby urged.

Joe looked through the binoculars at the trees outside. Every leaf seemed to be right under his nose. "Incredible!" Joe said. Then he handed back the binoculars.

Bobby grinned. He looked around the clubhouse. "Speaking of incredible, isn't it incredible in here?" he said. "I want to take a closer look around. Then I'll catch up with you guys again."

Bobby headed for the far wall, with Henrietta trailing behind him. When Bobby peered up at the pine ceiling, Henrietta did, too. When Bobby traced a hand down the soft pine wall, so did Henrietta. Finally, Bobby strode back to where Joe and David and Sam were standing. Henrietta was still at his heels.

"If I win this clubhouse, I'm going to make it into an observatory," Bobby said.

27

"If I win, that's just what I'm going to do, too," Henrietta declared.

"Henrietta, you don't even like the stars," Bobby said, exasperated. Henrietta grew silent and stared down at the clubhouse floor.

"Maybe you'd like to join our club, if we win the clubhouse," Joe said.

Bobby smiled. "I'd love to," he said. "I don't know a whole lot of people in Oakdale yet."

"I'd love to join also," said Henrietta.

Bobby looked more exasperated. "You had lots of friends your own age in our old neighborhood," Bobby said to Henrietta. "You should have them here, too. But you won't meet kids your own age if you hang around with me. If there's a club, I think it's a really bad idea for you to join. I don't think you should."

"Our old neighborhood was different. I knew those kids all my life," Henrietta said. She stepped back, looking miserable. Joe didn't know how a nine-year-old girl would fit in with the club, but he had to do something to make her feel better.

"You can join, too, Henrietta," Joe finally said.

Henrietta gave him a weak smile.

"Could I have your attention—" Wanda's voice filtered in through the open clubhouse door.

"I guess we had better head outside," Sam said. "The drawing should be soon."

Joe lingered at the door. He couldn't bring himself to step outside the clubhouse, because it might be forever. Wishbone suddenly nipped at his pants leg, tugging him forward.

Outside, a small crowd had gathered around

Wanda, who was holding her hands up for silence. Beside her, leaning casually against a tree, was Damont. Damont didn't look anxious, but Joe's heart was beating so hard he was certain everyone could hear it.

There was a smattering of applause. Wanda held up her hands again. "Thank you, thank you," she said. "I welcome you to the Oakdale Historical Society's raffling off of the clubhouse," she said. "This clubhouse has a lot of wonderful history to it. Built in the 1930s, it was first situated on what is now Forrest Lane. It was originally used as a clubhouse for the Oakdale Magicians' Club—isn't that magical? Later, in the 1940s, it was used as a clubhouse for the local Brownie troop. Then, when Forrest Lane was paved, the historical society decided to preserve it. Now, we've chosen to put it in what I feel is one of the loveliest spots in the park! Are we ready?"

Joe sucked in a deep breath. Wishbone shifted his weight from paw to paw.

Wanda dug her hand into the bowl. It disappeared all the way up to her elbow. Then she pulled out a strip of paper. She smiled. "Ladies and gentlemen, we have a winner!" she cried.

Henrietta held her hands up in the air and crossed her fingers tightly. Joe tried to calm his pounding heart. He swayed back and forth on the heels of his sneakers. His eyes darted in the direction of Mr. Pruitt, then at Mr. Barnes, and then, finally, at Damont. All of them wanted the clubhouse, maybe as much as Joe did. His hands were sweating at his sides.

"Joe Talbot!" cried Wanda.

Chapter Three

"I'm the winner!" Joe cried out, astonished. His heart was beating even faster now than it had been before the drawing. He looked at Sam, who was jumping up and down happily. Then he looked at David and Bobby, who were clapping wildly. Henrietta was laughing, and Wishbone was barking. In the distance, he could see his mother coming toward him, giving him a joyful victory salute. All around Joe was the noise of people clapping and cheering and calling his name. Joe stared at the clubhouse. It was really his! He had really won the grand prize! He bent and hugged Wishbone.

Sam and David gave him a quick hug. Mr. Pruitt and Mr. Barnes came over to shake Joe's hand. Emily looked shocked. "Can we get a recount?" she called. Damont just grinned and shrugged and acted as if he didn't want the clubhouse anyway. He began to walk away from the park.

Joe noticed that Henrietta looked really glum. Bobby was saying something to her in a low voice, and she was nodding her head, as if she had a headache that wasn't going away.

Wanda clapped for attention. "And now for the ribbon-cutting ceremony." She walked over to the clubhouse and pulled a blue ribbon out of her pocket. "I couldn't get the ribbon to stay tied around the clubhouse," she said. "So this is symbolic." She held up the ribbon and cut it in two. "The clubhouse is now officially yours," she said to Joe. She smiled. "Where are you going to put it?"

"In my backyard," Joe said happily.

"We'll load it on the truck and take it there right after everyone has some refreshments," Wanda said.

Ellen reached Joe's side. "I'm so thrilled that you won, Joe," Ellen said, and she gave him a big hug.

"Listen," Joe said to his friends, "let's all plan to meet at my house tomorrow. Right after school! And let's start decorating, too, making the clubhouse really be ours."

People began milling around the refreshment table, piling their paper plates with doughnuts and cake, and filling their cups with punch.

"I'm too excited to eat anything here," Joe said. He did take two pieces of yellow cake and feed some to Wishbone. Then he left the rest of the cake for Wishbone to eat at his leisure. Wishbone parked himself in front of his snack and licked his mouth clean after each delicious bite.

While he ate, Joe watched the truck driver getting into the truck, backing it closer to the clubhouse so he could load it on. The truck driver had three other men with him. One of the men was maneuvering the forklift, which had been removed from the back of the truck. All of a sudden the truck's engine abruptly sputtered and stopped. The driver got out, shaking his head.

"What's going on?" Joe asked.

The driver opened up the hood of the truck and looked underneath. Then he started walking over to Wanda, who was pouring the punch for the assembled group.

"Is something wrong?" Wanda asked.

"It's the oddest thing," he said to Wanda. "The truck was working fine all day. I just had it tuned up, but the engine won't turn over. I can't find anything wrong with it, either. I'm going to have to use my CB radio to call for a tow."

Joe looked alarmed. He came over and tapped the driver on the shoulder. "So I won't have the clubhouse tonight?" Joe asked.

"Doesn't look like it if the truck won't start," the driver said. "But don't worry, it's probably nothing. I'm sure the clubhouse will be in your backyard by the time you get home from school tomorrow."

Wanda put one hand on Joe's shoulder. He stared longingly at the clubhouse and wished that tomorrow didn't seem so very far away.

The crowd began to go home. People grabbed one last muffin, took a final look at the clubhouse, then left the park. Joe walked his bike to the parking lot and said good-bye to his mother and Wanda.

As Joe rode home on his bike, with Wishbone trotting alongside him, he kept thinking about the clubhouse and his father's mysteries. He couldn't wait for the clubhouse to be delivered. But he also was just as eager to get home and start reading his dad's favorite books.

That night after dinner, Joe picked up the Agatha Christie volume and settled back to read. Wishbone chewed a toy at his feet. Just picking up the mystery made Joe think of his father again. Joe imagined his father reading this very same book, maybe even in this very same chair.

Joe didn't know what to expect when he began to read the Agatha Christie book, but after the first few pages, he was hooked! Ten different people were housed on this island, and yet the host was nowhere to be found. None of the guests knew one another, but each one seemed to have something to hide. There were ten little Indian figurines sitting on a table in the big old mansion's dining room. One of the figurines would disappear, and then shortly afterward, a guest would mysteriously die. Something very strange was happening at the gloomy old house, and Joe wanted to read more of the suspenseful tale to find out what it was. *It's just like something very strange is going on with that tow truck,* Joe thought.

As Joe became more and more involved in his reading, Wishbone began to feel restless, right down to his four paws. "Joe, I think I'll take a walk. I'll be back soon." Wishbone made his "Let me out, please" sound, a deep bark. Then, for added emphasis, he went to the front door and scratched at it.

"At your service," Joe said, getting up and walking to the door. He opened it up and waited for Wishbone to go outside. "See you later, Wishbone," Joe said.

Wishbone stepped outside. He walked through the neighborhood briskly, enjoying the cool night air. He trotted along Forrest Lane searching for any interesting object he could find, like a ball, when he noticed a new scent in the air. "Tuna," Wishbone said. He lifted his head and sniffed. "Equal parts tuna and fur ball—it's cat!" He turned. "This could be great practice for the cat-chasing invitational contest next week! I could take time out from my search."

Wishbone turned a corner. On the sidewalk by the road he called Danger Lane, because of all the traffic there, was a group of four large cats.

"A feast of felines," Wishbone said, preparing to give chase. Just then, one of the cats reared back, and Wishbone saw that in the center of the group was a tiny black kitten. "Oh, a pint-sized pest," Wishbone said. The kitten mewed, and one of the cats batted at her, claws drawn. Wishbone noticed how the other cats were all attacking the kitten and menacing her, batting her with their paws, hissing and snarling. Wishbone was upset to see such bad behavior. "It's just a kitten, you big fur-heads," he scolded.

Two of the cats yowled.

"What on earth are they saying?" Wishbone said. "I don't speak Cat. I never liked the sound of that language." Wishbone shook his head. "My Dogspeak is so much more musical." Wishbone squinted in the darkness. "I haven't seen this little one before. I'll bet it's a stray."

Just then, two of the cats batted the little kitten

again, making it cry in fear. Another large cat sneaked up on the kitten from behind and scratched it hard.

"Hey, cut that out!" Wishbone said. "Pick on someone your own size! I see plenty of cats here who could use a good scratch!" Wishbone's fur bristled.

Then, the cat scratched at the kitten again. This time, Wishbone couldn't help himself. Cat or no cat, he had to do something. And fast. Wishbone barked loudly, scattering the cats, including the kitten. Unfortunately, the kitten ran into the middle of the street. A car zoomed by, honking so loudly that Wishbone winced. But the kitten stood in the middle of the road, frozen in fear.

"You dummy," Wishbone said. "Run!" The kitten looked at him. Another car zoomed by. Wishbone hesitated. He was the one who had chased the cat right into Danger Lane. Wishbone had heard terrible stories about what had happened to dogs who just ran out into that road. You had to be careful. You had to look both ways and then wait until there were no cars around at all.

The kitten mewed piteously. Another car came by, and Wishbone couldn't stand it any longer. He had to do something! He braced himself. *Careful, careful,* he told himself. There were two cars coming—a red one and a blue one. They were far enough apart so he could dash into the road after the red car just passed by and grab the kitten before the blue car came. Wishbone finally ran out into the road and plucked the kitten up into his mouth.

"Yuck! I hate the taste of cat fur," he said. With the kitten in his mouth, he dashed into the nearby park. He set the little cat down on a soft, grassy patch.

"Okay, the coast is clear. Now, scat, cat!" He rubbed at his mouth with his paw. "Oh, this tastes strange." He looked at the cat. "Dog rules say that if a cat is too small, I have to throw you back. Like fishing," he said. The kitten looked up at him with adoring eyes. "Oh, no, you don't," Wishbone said. "Just because I saved you doesn't mean I like you."

The whole way home, Wishbone tried to lose the kitten, who insisted on trailing behind him.

"Come on, this is strange," he said to the kitten. "Cats don't love dogs. It's all part of the rules." The kitten purred even louder than before. Wishbone sighed. *I'll try to do dog-type things, so maybe this kitty will get the hint,* Wishbone thought. He ran through muddy areas, but the kitten gingerly followed him, picking its way through the mud. He chased a big blue station wagon, nearly catching it. He veered around and saw the kitten was in the road, too, following him, trying to keep up. The kitten was out of breath, but it

36

wasn't panting the elegant way dogs did. Well, if the little ball of fur was tired, that could be Wishbone's chance to make a break for it. He knew cats were lazier than dogs. They didn't romp the way dogs did. And a cat wouldn't exert itself, especially if it was already tired. Wishbone put his four paws into high gear and bounded back toward the park. He waited until he was on the grass before he turned around. The cat was gone!

This is the way I like my day to end, Wishbone thought, *with no cat around!* Then he trotted back toward home. He couldn't wait for tomorrow. The clubhouse would arrive. The one thing that would make the clubhouse perfect was a "No Cats Allowed" sign.

Chapter Four

The next day Joe was furiously bicycling home from school. Sam and Bobby and David were following him as fast as they could. All that morning, Joe hadn't been able to concentrate in his classes. The only thing he could think about was that when he got home, the clubhouse would be in his backyard, just waiting for all of them. He could picture it in his mind. The clubhouse would be set back toward his favorite big tree, so the shade would keep it cool during the summer. He'd keep the front door of the clubhouse facing the back door of his house. "I hope they put the clubhouse in the right spot, by the big tree," Joe said, out of breath.

"I can't wait to see it," Sam said.

Everyone had brought something for the clubhouse. Sam carried her Polaroid camera to take pictures of it. David was donating a portable radio. Even Wishbone had dug out his favorite blue ball that morning from under the living room couch. He brought it to the backyard, where he would place it, along with other objects, inside the clubhouse.

"We're here!" Joe cried, speeding the final distance toward his house. He slowed down to a halt and got off his bike, setting it down on the lawn. "And there's Wishbone!" Joe looked up at his front porch.

Wishbone was lying down, his paws over his face. His tail wagged weakly. Joe felt a pang of worry. Wishbone usually bounded up to meet him, his tail held high, his ears perked up. This wasn't like him at all! Joe went up to the porch and bent down to examine Wishbone to make sure he wasn't sick. His nose felt cold and his fur had an odd shiny look to it. Wishbone licked Joe's hand, almost as if he were trying to comfort his human pal.

"Henrietta must be in the backyard already," Bobby said. "She only had a half day at her school today." He shook his head. "I told her not to come, but she got so upset—"

"Look, she can come over if she wants to," Joe said.

Bobby shook his head. "It's for her own good. She's got to meet kids her own age. She won't do that if she hangs around with us."

Joe stood up. Maybe Wishbone was just feeling lonely waiting for them. He bet Wishbone would feel better when they all went out back into the clubhouse. "Come on. Last one to get to the backyard is a rotten egg!" Joe shouted.

They raced to the backyard. Joe's heart was hammering with excitement. When he got to the backyard, he stopped so short that Sam nearly tumbled into him. There was the big tree that was going to give them shade all through the summer. There were Ellen's rosebushes. But there was no clubhouse!

"What's going on?" Bobby asked.

Just then the back door opened and Ellen and Henrietta came out. Ellen had her arm around the little girl's shoulders. "I'm sorry, kids," Ellen said. "Wanda called a little while ago. The driver of the truck says there's something wrong with the transmission. He has to order some parts. It's going to take a few more days for the clubhouse to be delivered."

Wishbone stood close to Joe. "A few more days!" Joe exclaimed. "Can't they get another truck?"

"The historical society already paid this trucker," Ellen said.

Wishbone sat on the grass and buried his head in his paws. He looked to Joe as if he was as disappointed as everybody else was.

"I was really looking forward to this," Bobby said.

Ellen looked sympathetic. "Aren't you all forgetting something? The clubhouse is still yours. You can still have your club meetings in it. You just have to go to Jackson Park to do it for now." She smiled. "It's only temporary."

Joe felt as if a weight was lifting from his shoulders. His mother was right. He began to feel a little better about things. It didn't matter if they had to visit the clubhouse in the park. It was still their clubhouse.

He looked up at the sky. It was still light out. They could get to the park and spend a few hours there.

"Let's go," Sam said enthusiastically.

Wishbone picked up his ball, making Joe laugh. "Even Wishbone's ready," he said.

"I'll see you for supper, Joe," Ellen said. "All of you, have a good time. You, too, Wishbone."

The kids got on their bicycles and headed for the park—and the clubhouse.

Joe pedaled as fast as he could. The only sound to be heard was the whirr of bicycle tires as the kids pedaled frantically to get to Jackson Park. Even Wishbone was running at top dog-speed. The closer Joe got to the clubhouse, the better he felt. By the time he saw the clubhouse itself, standing there, all gray, weathered pine in the bright late-afternoon light, he was smiling. The kids slowed their bikes and then parked them on the grass by the clubhouse.

Wishbone darted around the clubhouse, barking happily.

Without all the people around, or the truck, or the table of refreshments, the clubhouse looked as if it had always been in Jackson Park. "It's so beautiful!" Sam said, stepping inside once again. The others followed her. The interior felt cool, and it was quiet and peaceful. The late-afternoon sunshine came in through the windows, casting a golden glow on patches of the pine walls and floor.

"This is wonderful," Bobby said.

Sam looked around. "Can't you just feel it?" she asked. "There's a kind of power in here. It's from all the people who must have sat in here and had their club meetings here. It goes all the way back to the 1930s. Just imagine—there were even other kids like us in here years ago."

Wishbone barked. "And dogs like you," Joe said.

The kids settled on the floor. Bobby crossed his arms. Henrietta immediately crossed hers, too. David ran one hand along the floor. "I think I should be in

41

charge of taking care of the wood so that it will continue to resist rain and stuff."

"Are we all going to have jobs?" said Henrietta.

"Well, we could," Joe said. "Like president, secretary—that sort of thing."

"You should be president, because you won the clubhouse," Sam said to Joe.

Wishbone barked. "Oh, and Wishbone can be our club mascot," Joe said.

"I can be chief technical engineer," David said. "If something breaks, I'll fix it."

"I'll be the club chef. I'll supply the chips and pretzels and stuff," Bobby said.

Wishbone perked up and edged near Bobby. Wishbone's movements didn't surprise Joe. He knew snacks were in Wishbone's blood.

"Wait! You all forgot me! Don't leave me out! What can I be?" asked Henrietta urgently.

"Club pest," Bobby said.

Henrietta grew silent.

"You can be the club lookout, Henrietta," Sam said kindly.

"What am I looking out for?" she asked.

"I don't know. People. Animals," Sam said.

"Animals! I like that," Henrietta said. Henrietta bent down and rubbed Wishbone behind his ears, exactly the way Joe knew Wishbone liked to be stroked. Wishbone lifted one paw and rested it on Henrietta's free arm, almost as if the two were already the best of friends.

"What should we do first?" Bobby asked.

"I know—let's take some group pictures with my

instant camera," Sam said. "We can frame them and hang them in the clubhouse."

Joe loved the idea of taking pictures. It would be like freezing this exciting moment in time. He could look at them and remember just how happy he was right that very minute, with all his friends around, in the clubhouse. All the kids stood up and began to search around for the best place to pose. Joe looked over at the far window where the most light came in. "How about there?" he asked, pointing. The kids went over to the window and stood closely together. Wishbone settled himself at Joe's feet.

"Let me set the timer on this thing," Sam said, fiddling with the dial. She carefully set the camera on the opposite window ledge and then hurried over to join the group. "One—two—three— Say 'clubhouse,'" Sam instructed.

"Clubhouse!" they cried together, as the camera clicked and flashed.

Wishbone barked. "That's 'clubhouse' in dog language," Joe said. Sam laughed and went to get her camera. She counted out the seconds and then finally pulled the picture out from the slot in the back.

"Let's see! Let's see!" Henrietta called.

Joe moved toward Sam. Sam frowned. She stared intently at the picture and then looked up. "This is really strange," she said. "Look at this, guys."

She held up the picture. The photograph showed them all smiling, all posing, but above them, in the window, was a shadowy face!

"Do you see what I see?" Sam asked. "I didn't see

anything like that when I set up the camera to take the picture."

Joe was startled. He stared at the picture. It looked just like a face wearing a mask! He stepped back and looked again. This time, it seemed as if it could be just a shadow. "Maybe it's nothing," he said weakly.

"Maybe it's just an optical illusion," Bobby said.

"Let me take another look," Joe said. He took the photo from Sam. Sure enough, in the window behind them was a face! It was in shadows, so it wasn't possible to tell who it really was. But Joe could see eyes and a nose and an unsmiling mouth. He couldn't see the hair at all, or any clothing. He couldn't even see the rest of the body! Joe suddenly felt nervous, as if someone—or something—was watching them.

"Someone must have been outside," Bobby decided. "Let's go outside and check it out." He strode out first, his arms swinging. Henrietta struggled to keep up with him.

They all walked outside, closing the door to the clubhouse firmly. Joe couldn't shake off his feeling of uneasiness. He told himself it was scarier not to know what was going on than to know, and the thing to do was to get to the truth.

The group all walked close together.

"Who's there?" Sam called. "Is someone there? Show yourself."

Wishbone began to sniff and paw at the ground.

"Anybody there?" Joe called.

"I'm scared," Henrietta said.

"Maybe you should go home," Bobby said. "This is no place for a little kid."

Henrietta grew suddenly quiet. "I'll go wait inside the clubhouse," she said in a small voice. She turned and then started to walk away.

"Let's look in those bushes over there," Sam said, pointing to tall hedges by a nearby path. She walked over, pushing aside the bushes with her hands.

David peered over at the trees. Bobby got down on his hands and knees and tried to see if anyone was crouched down in the bushes, hiding.

Suddenly Henrietta was back. She started to tug at Bobby's sleeve. "Bobby—" she said. "Bobby—"

Bobby crawled deeper into the bushes. "Wait just a second. I want to look in these bushes—" he said.

"Bobby!" Henrietta said loudly. She tugged on him so roughly that he turned to face her. Silently, she pointed one trembling finger. "Look!" she said. "Everybody, look!"

They all turned to see where she was pointing. Joe's mouth dropped open.

The clubhouse door, which they had shut firmly, was now wide open, and a strange voice was booming, *"Get Out!"*

Chapter Five

"*Get out!*" the voice boomed again. Then the door slammed shut. A chill crept up Joe's spine. Every muscle in his body urged him to run. He felt frozen in place. But he couldn't just run away. This was his clubhouse. He had to find out what was going on. Who was telling them to get out? And why?

"Let's get away from here!" Henrietta cried.

"No. I'm going to find out who's in there," Joe said firmly.

"Let's all go," Sam said.

They all walked slowly toward the clubhouse. Joe felt his heart beating faster. *Every mystery has a solution,* he told himself.

Joe walked right up to the clubhouse. He took a deep breath and then opened the door. He wasn't sure what he expected to find. Inside, everything looked exactly the same as it always had. There were the same gray pine walls, the same three tiny windows. Wishbone walked in and sniffed around in all the corners. Then even he gave up and sat down in the middle of

the clubhouse, shaking his head as if to say he couldn't figure out what was going on, either.

Henrietta lagged behind. "Where did that voice come from?" she whispered. "Do you think it was a ghost?"

"A ghost?" Joe said. "There's no such thing as ghosts." He put his hand down and petted Wishbone, which always made him feel calmer. He didn't want to tell anyone that he was secretly afraid of ghosts. In fact, he didn't like to go past the old Murphy house because it made him feel so nervous. No one lived there anymore. It was falling apart and it looked just like the kind of place ghosts would frequent—if you believed in ghosts.

He wasn't going to give in to superstition now, not when there was something as important as his clubhouse at stake. His father used to try to solve mysteries all the time. Maybe this time, Joe could, too. He sucked in a deep breath. Beside him, Wishbone sighed.

"Maybe someone's just playing a joke on us," Joe said.

"I don't care. This is creepy," Henrietta said. "Someone doesn't want us to be here. Let's go."

Joe looked uncertain. "There has to be a logical explanation—I mean, maybe someone is standing someplace where we can't see him."

"Maybe we can find what we're looking for—tomorrow. But let's get out of here now," Henrietta said.

"All right, all right," Joe said. He was suddenly glad it was starting to get dark, so no one could see just how nervous he really was. The entire group went outside the clubhouse.

David checked the door, opening and closing it. "As my first job as technical manager, I'll install a latch with a combination lock tomorrow. We can memorize the combination. That way no one will be able to get in except us."

"I'll check behind the clubhouse," Bobby offered, and he raced around the corner. When he came back to the front again, he was out of breath. "No sign of anyone anywhere."

"Let's go home," Joe said.

Wishbone was quiet as he walked home. It upset him when Joe was worried like this. He could smell Joe's anxiety in the air. His worry gave off a sharp tingle that tickled Wishbone's nose. Wishbone could tell, too, just how concerned Joe was by the way he was biking. His shoulders were hunched. His grip on the handlebars was so tight that his knuckles were white. He stared into space. "I wish I could perk you up, Joe," Wishbone said.

All of the kids were almost back at Joe's house when they ran across Wanda, coming toward them, her arms full of groceries. Wishbone felt his own spirits start to lift.

"Wanda, how considerate of you to shop for me," Wishbone said. "Did you remember the ginger snaps?"

The kids slowed down on their bikes, finally coming to a stop so they could say hello to Wanda.

"You kids look anxious," Wanda said. She paused. "Did Ellen tell you it's going to take another day or so to get the parts for the truck? I just called the driver again. It was the strangest thing. The dealer didn't have a few simple parts in stock." She stopped talking suddenly. "You all look so peculiar. What's going on?"

"The clubhouse is haunted!" Henrietta cried out.

"It is not," Joe insisted. "Someone's just playing a joke on us."

"We saw this weird figure in a picture we took—" Henrietta said breathlessly. "And we heard a strange, creepy voice yelling at us to get out—"

"Henrietta—" Bobby said. "She gets carried away," he said to Wanda.

"I do not," Henrietta insisted. "There was a weird figure in that picture."

"Really?" Wanda looked intrigued. "Can I see that photo?" she asked.

Sam pulled it out of her pocket.

Wanda squinted at it. "That is strange," she admitted. "It almost looks like a face, doesn't it?"

"It could be something else," Joe insisted.

Wanda shrugged, giving the photo back to Sam. "You know, I have a book inside about ghosts. Maybe we should take a look at it." Wanda shifted the bag of groceries on her hip. "Boy, these groceries are heavy," she said.

"Lighten your load a little, Wanda," Wishbone said. "I'll take some things off your hands. Like that hamburger meat I smell. It's there right on top. You can reach it without even trying."

"Ghosts?" Joe repeated, echoing Wanda's remark.

Wanda turned to go inside.

51

"Wait just a minute! The book is fiction, right?" Wishbone called.

The kids sat in Wanda's living room, while Wanda peered at her bookshelf. Joe didn't like the idea of Wanda's ghost book one single bit. He thought it would make the situation even worse.

"Here it is," she said. "*Ghosts of America.* What a great book!" She pulled it down and opened it up on her coffee table.

"There is no ghost," Joe insisted.

But no one else seemed to be listening to him. Sam was poring over the book. Bobby was hunched forward excitedly. David, too, was gently touching the faded blue cover of the book, examining the gold-trimmed pages.

"Here it is," Wanda said, pointing to a page and reading. "'The Oakdale ghost is supposedly the spirit of a little girl named Amanda Blake, who lived in Oakdale in 1890 and loved to go into Jackson Park to pick wild-flowers. One day she went picking and never returned. The whole town gathered together to search for her. Her parents offered a huge reward to anyone who could provide information about her disappearance. It was said she had been kidnapped, but there were no suspects. And no one ever found her. Her family left town soon after that. It is said that on some nights you can hear Amanda crying in the woods, and there is one patch of land in the park where no wildflowers have ever grown again.'"

"Do you think that patch of land is where our clubhouse is now?" Bobby asked.

"It doesn't say," Wanda said. "I suppose it could be." She leafed ahead a couple of pages. There were no maps in the book.

"Do you think the Oakdale ghost is in our club-house? Maybe she's upset that something was put on her land," Henrietta said. She reached over and petted Wishbone. "Do you think the ghost likes dogs?"

Joe began to feel even more uneasy than he had been before Wanda told them of the Oakdale ghost. He wanted everyone to find the clues to this mystery and solve them. He didn't want them talking about ghosts as if they really existed. He stepped back from the book. "Every mystery has a solution," he blurted out.

"Then what's the solution to this one?" Sam said.

"I don't know," Joe said. "But I'm reading this mystery book of my father's. Maybe what I come across in there can help us solve this." He suddenly got excited. He hadn't thought the mystery book might help with this problem.

"The book was your father's?" Sam asked.

Joe nodded. "It's really great, too. It's called *Ten Little Indians*. Anyway, I can't figure out the mystery in my book, either. But I will before I get to the end of the story!"

Wanda looked thoughtful. "I have a solution," she said.

Thank goodness, Joe thought. Wanda was an adult, and although sometimes her ideas seemed a little off the wall to Joe, he liked and trusted her. He thought maybe she really could come up with a solution that would put things in a whole different light. The other kids were looking at her with a sense of respect, which meant they would listen to her.

Wanda smiled. "We should talk to the ghost. We need to find out why the ghost is haunting the clubhouse. Then we can try to figure out what we can do to get her to stop upsetting everyone," Wanda said.

Joe's face fell.

"Excuse me?" said Bobby.

"I'm talking about having what's called a séance," Wanda said. "A group of people gather in a circle. You join hands, concentrate, and you communicate with the spirits. You find out what they want, try to provide what they need, and then they go away."

"Oh, great," Joe said, sinking down into a chair. Wishbone leaped up into his lap, licking his face, but the terrier's good intentions didn't make Joe feel much better. A séance! And Joe had hoped Wanda might be on his side, and refuse to admit ghosts even existed. But it sure didn't seem that way. What was even worse was that the other kids were listening to Wanda!

"You talk, and the ghosts talk back," Wanda explained. "Actually, they don't really *talk,* not the way we do. They *communicate*—they sometimes do this by rapping on the wall or making objects move."

Sam looked doubtful.

"Ghosts are like living people," Wanda said. "Sometimes they're just lonely and they want attention. So you acknowledge them and say hello once in a while and they stop haunting. Or sometimes they want you to give a message to someone who they left behind in the world of the living."

"I don't think this is such a good idea," Joe said.

"Oh, come on," Sam said. "Maybe it will work. And it could be fun."

"You said you didn't believe in ghosts," Bobby said to Joe. "So what harm could it do to go along with Ms. Gilmore's idea to have a séance? And maybe it could help." He grew thoughtful. "I think we should be scientific about this. Test out the idea. Maybe we should record the séance. Or take pictures. I'll bring my binoculars so we can see the ghost clearly!" He grinned.

Joe felt grumpy. He didn't want to have a séance! And certainly not in his clubhouse. "We don't know anyone who could conduct a séance, anyway," he said.

Wanda smiled. "Oh, yes, you do," she said. "And *I* can lead it for you—oh, say, tomorrow afternoon!"

Chapter Six

Tomorrow afternoon! Joe thought. The other kids gathered excitedly around Wanda. They were so caught up with the idea of a séance that they didn't seem to hear Joe saying good-bye. They didn't seem to notice Joe quietly leaving, with Wishbone following faithfully behind him. Joe biked glumly home from Wanda's, Wishbone trotting by his side. He couldn't believe it! Everyone really *wanted* the séance—everyone but him. They actually thought it would be fun.

Joe needed to calm down. He parked his bike in his driveway near the garage and went inside his house. The séance was scheduled for four o'clock tomorrow. He just wanted to forget the whole thing. Joe walked into the house, right when Ellen came into the room.

"Hi, Joe. Hi, Wishbone," Ellen said. She studied Joe and frowned. "What's wrong?"

Joe slumped into a chair. "Everyone thought they saw a mysterious face in a picture Sam took in the clubhouse. We ran into Ms. Gilmore on the way home, and she thinks the clubhouse is haunted. She's going to conduct a séance there tomorrow afternoon!"

"A séance!" Ellen said. She sat down beside Joe. "Well, that doesn't mean the clubhouse is haunted."

"No," Joe said thoughtfully, "I guess not."

"Think of it as a new experience. A séance could be fun," Ellen said.

"Fun—right," Joe said. "That's what the other kids said." He sighed. "I think I'm going to read some more. That will take my mind off it."

Ellen smiled at him. She stood up and ruffled his hair, then left the room. Joe leaned over toward the table where his Agatha Christie book was. He settled in to read, opening up the volume. In minutes, he was absorbed in the story. The more he read of this book, the more curious he was to find out what would happen next.

Now another Indian figurine had disappeared, and soon after that, another guest had died! The remaining guests now decided that their host, who was nowhere to be found, must somehow be behind the awful events occurring in the dreary old seaside mansion. They were about to explore the island to try to find the host. They were going to demand an explanation for what was going on. Some of the guests even thought the host was the one who was killing off the guests.

Joe thoughtfully tapped his fingers on the open book. The host was a *real* flesh-and-blood person, not a ghost. Joe suddenly sat up straighter. The clubhouse ghost could be a *real* person, too. But who? In the book, the characters were all sure there was a solution to the mystery.

Wishbone snuggled up next to Joe. The séance was going to take place just for fun, Joe told himself. They would have the séance tomorrow, as scheduled, and then everyone would forget about it.

Wishbone was resting on the sidewalk at Joe's school, waiting for the day's classes to end. When Joe finally came out, he looked glum. He was walking so slowly that Wishbone wondered for a moment if they would ever get home. And once Joe got there, Wishbone wondered if they would ever leave. Again, Joe took his time after he got in the house. Ellen was working at the library, so Joe and Wishbone sat alone at the kitchen table. Joe helped himself to two glasses of milk and four vanilla cookies.

"Uh . . . excuse me, did you forget something?" Wishbone asked, standing on his hind legs as his front paws slowly moved along the edge of the table, feeling around for a couple of tasty crumbs.

Joe gave him a cookie, and Wishbone swallowed it down in a flash. He didn't like to waste food, not even a single scrap. Wishbone adored cookies, but he loved Joe more, and he didn't like to see his pal so unsettled.

Finally, Joe sighed and began to go outside, where he had parked his bike. He held the door open for Wishbone. "Time to go," Joe said.

Joe pedaled so slowly that Wishbone was barely getting any exercise. Every once in a while Wishbone barked, trying to make Joe step up his pace so that he would feel better. Joe just sighed. Wishbone bounded ahead a bit.

Finally, they arrived at the park. Wishbone could see David in the distance. He was outside the clubhouse, busily installing a latch and a combination lock on the door. All the other kids' bikes were parked outside. David looked up when he saw Joe and grinned, pointing to the lock.

"There," he said, finishing up. "Now no one can get in here unless they know the combination. It's twenty-two to the right, twenty-two to the left, fourteen to the right. It's a good precaution to have this lock—just in case what's been spooking us isn't a ghost." David dusted his hands off on his pants. "Ms. Gilmore's just about to start. Let's go inside."

Wishbone went inside first. Instantly, he smelled a strange aroma, something even his keen nose couldn't place. He looked around. None of the other kids seemed to be bothered by it. They were all sitting in a circle in the center of the floor. David and Joe sat down and joined them.

Wanda stood in the center of the circle. She didn't look quite like the Wanda Wishbone was accustomed to seeing. She was wearing a big silvery turban that completely covered the top of her head and all of her hair. The odd-looking hat had fringe hanging from it, and a silvery fan stuck out on top. Lots of big bangle bracelets covered her arms, and they jangled almost musically every time she moved. She wore a pair of earrings as large as small bones. The sweater she had wrapped around her sparkled with tiny sequins. Wanda was holding a small glass that had something

burning inside it. She rotated it slowly in a circle. The substance gave off a sharp smell that made Wishbone put his paws over his nose.

"Yikes!" he said. "Did something die in here?"

"What's that smell?" Joe said, sniffing.

"I think I just discovered the one thing—whatever it is—that could ruin my appetite," Wishbone said.

"Shh!" said Wanda, moving the glass in a circle one more time. "It's sage—an herb. I burned a little to rid the clubhouse of any bad spirits. Ghosts can't stand the smell of sage."

"Neither can dogs," Wishbone added.

Wanda sighed. She stopped moving the glass, blew out the burning sage, and sat down. Instantly, the clubhouse seemed more quiet than it had ever been before. The candle Wanda had placed in the center of the circle gave off an eerie glow. It cast shadows on the walls that flickered and moved and seemed almost alive. There was no sound but the whoosh of the wind outside and the breathing of all the kids as they nervously waited for Wanda to proceed.

Wishbone lifted his head and tried to sniff out any ghosts. His fur stiffened along his back. He moved closer to Joe. "I'll guard you, Joe," he said, but even he began to feel a little unsure of himself. He had tangled with cats and other dogs, and cars, but never with a ghost. He didn't know what he was supposed to do if a real ghost actually showed up!

"Now, at this séance we are going to try to speak to the spirit of the Oakdale ghost!" Wanda said. She dramatically raised her hands. "We must all be very quiet and concentrate."

Wishbone drew himself up. Maybe the ghost was a dog. A good dog. Like Rin Tin Tin. Or Lassie. He felt himself brightening. Dog-ghosts like that could even help him. He bet they would know exactly what to do about an annoying little kitten that stuck to them like glue.

Wanda shut her eyes. "Hold hands," she instructed. Everybody did as they were told. Wishbone stayed close to Joe, putting one paw on Joe's arm. "Now shut your eyes and concentrate." Wishbone shut his eyes. Wanda began to hum and then to speak. "Oh, mighty Oakdale ghost, if you are around, make yourself known. Show yourself to us."

"Wait a minute," Wishbone said. "Can't the ghost just send us a postcard? Does it have to *appear?*"

"Tell us what to do to make you happy so you will leave the clubhouse," Wanda said.

"You feel anything?" Sam whispered to Joe.

Joe shook his head no.

"My side is itching," Wishbone said, and he scratched it with his hind leg.

"Make yourself known, Amanda," Wanda sang.

She rocked her body back and forth. Again, there was silence. The air seemed to hum around them. Wishbone looked up at one of the windows. Light still streamed in. The sky still shone blue.

"Sometimes the spirits communicate by knocks or with patterns of light. They don't always speak," Wanda whispered. She pointed to the wall where a patch of light was flickering. "That could be a spirit," she said. Henrietta suddenly seemed nervous, and she let go of Joe's hand. Wanda leaned over calmly and

moved Henrietta's hand back into Joe's. "And sometimes they speak through a willing person."

Bobby coughed.

Wanda looked up abruptly.

Bobby coughed again, then sneezed.

"Well, that could just be a cold," Wanda admitted.

Henrietta looked even more alarmed. She again
jerked her hands free from her partners in the circle,
but Wanda leaned forward and quickly put them back
into place.

"You mustn't break the chain!" Wanda warned.
"It makes the spirits angry!"

Wanda shut her eyes, humming, louder and
louder. She rocked her body back and forth. She tugged
at Sam's hand on her left, and Bobby's hand on her
right, making them move with her.

"Speak!" she commanded.

Wishbone heard the command and almost barked
before he remembered that it was a ghost Wanda
wanted to speak, and not him. Wishbone settled back
down, tipping over a chair.

Instantly, Henrietta jumped. "It's the ghost!" she
cried.

Wanda looked over at Wishbone. "Sorry, my
mistake," Wishbone said.

"No, that was just the dog." Wanda said. "But listen
carefully. Ghosts make odd sounds sometimes. Like
trumpets. Or like whispers. Sometimes they can even
drop things out of the sky right into your lap." Wanda
shut her eyes one more time. "Give us a sign!" she
commanded.

The clubhouse was so still that Wishbone felt

unnerved. He sniffed at the air, trying to sense if anything smelled different. Nope. He could only smell wood and humans and dog.

Wanda opened her eyes and looked around the clubhouse. She squinted and stared, and then finally she sighed. She broke the chain of hands, standing up. "Guys," she said solemnly, "and girls," she added, nodding at Sam and Henrietta, "I'm sorry, but due to the lack of cooperation on the ghost's part, this séance is officially over."

Joe opened his eyes, and then so did Sam and David and Bobby and Henrietta. All of the kids looked at one another.

"People, there's only one explanation for why this didn't work," Wanda said.

"It's because there is no ghost," Joe said.

"I don't care that it didn't work. It was fun," Sam said happily.

Wanda shook her head. "The ghost is *shy,*" she explained. "Why don't you make her feel at home—talk to her, put her at ease."

"Do you think she likes kibble?" Wishbone asked.

"We don't want a ghost!" Sam said.

"Well," Wanda said, "you might have one."

"Everyone thought something supernatural was going on in my book, *Ten Little Indians,* too," Joe said suddenly. "But all the crazy things were being done by a real person. It's possible that our ghost is a real person, too."

"Could be," said Wanda. "You could explore that idea some more."

"But who could it be?" said Bobby.

"Yeah. Who?" Henrietta demanded.

"Don't look at the dog," said Wishbone. "I don't have a *motive,* which, as we say in the mystery biz, is a reason for doing something."

"Every mystery has suspects," Joe said.

"But who are our suspects?" Sam asked.

"Who else wanted the clubhouse?" Joe asked.

"Just about everyone in Oakdale bought a ticket for the raffle," Sam said.

"Mr. Pruitt really wanted it for a writing studio," David said. "But I can't see him haunting a clubhouse."

"Mr. Barnes wanted the clubhouse to use as a playhouse for Emily," Sam said. "But he's a really nice man. He wouldn't do such a frightening thing to us. And Emily is too young to be causing us all of these problems."

Joe looked up. "Damont wanted to charge admission—" he said. Joe suddenly looked at Sam, who looked at David, who looked at Bobby, who looked at Henrietta.

"Damont!" they all cried in unison.

Damont! Wishbone should have guessed it. Damont had never been particularly friendly to Wishbone, which made the Damonster very, very suspect in Wishbone's book.

"So we all sort of think Damont is doing the haunting. But we can't just accuse him out of thin air. There is such a thing as being innocent until proven guilty," Bobby said.

Wishbone wagged his tail in agreement. "Yeah," said the terrier, "like you can't say for sure that it was me who played tag with Ellen's slippers."

"Damont!" Sam said. "It makes perfect sense. He wanted to have the clubhouse for himself, and now he's trying to scare us out of using it."

"How can we catch him at it, though?" Henrietta asked breathlessly.

"Well, in the book that I'm reading at home, the people look for evidence," Joe said. "They follow one another and see if anyone is acting suspiciously or doing anything out of the ordinary." He suddenly brightened. "That's it! We'll search the clubhouse for clues tomorrow. Damont may come out here late at night, after we've already left. We can follow Damont around town, too, and try to catch him doing something suspicious! It's a real-life mystery we all can solve."

Wishbone barked. "You lead, I'll follow."

"We can start tomorrow," Joe said. "First, we can all check out the clubhouse, and then Wishbone and I will start to tail Damont!" Joe said.

Chapter Seven

Wishbone ran beside all the kids and Wanda, as they all bicycled home from Jackson Park. He enjoyed the exercise. He also liked to see that each of his friends got home safely. It made him feel good right down to his whiskers.

They were just beginning to approach Joe's house, when suddenly Wishbone caught a familiar scent hanging in the air. He sniffed again, and suddenly he knew just what it was. It was as plain as the cold, wet nose on his face. It was small. It was furry. It was annoying. "Wishbone radar on alert!" he called. "Cat in the area! Sound the alarm! Cat!" Wishbone went into his high-alert barking mode. "I can smell it, but I can't see it."

"Hey! What's the matter, Wishbone?" Joe asked.

"Does he sense a ghost?" Wanda said. "Dogs are sensitive to things like that."

"It's worse than a ghost—it's a *cat!*" Wishbone said. "I'm being haunted by a *cat!*"

Wanda looked down. "Oh, look!" she said.

Wishbone turned around. There, following almost right behind him, was the kitten he had saved. It looked tired and hungry. It wobbled on its four paws, giving Wishbone a worshipful look. "Go away," Wishbone said. "Some things go together, like dogs and food, me and Joe—but never, ever do cats and dogs go together."

Wishbone noticed how Wanda's whole face lit up when she saw the kitten. Her eyes sparkled, as if seeing the kitten was something wonderful. It was one thing to see Wanda react in such a way, but to see Joe go wide-eyed at the creature was quite another matter. Wishbone looked worriedly over at Joe, who was also smiling at the kitten.

"She followed me home, and no, I certainly do not want to keep her!" Wishbone said. He glowered at the kitten, who hesitated and froze. "Don't touch her! You don't know where she's been!"

Joe got off his bike and bent down to stroke the cat, much to Wishbone's dismay.

"Here, kitty," Wanda said, as she got off her bike. She hoisted the cat up and held it in her arms. "Oh, what a sweetie pie."

"Don't do it, Wanda! Don't be fooled by fur!"

Wishbone said. "You want fur? Then take a good look at this season's latest style." He twisted this way and that, showing off his many good sides. "And not a flea on me!"

"This cat's a beauty," Wanda said. "Look how silky her coat is. I haven't seen her in the neighborhood before. But she looks too well cared for to be a stray. She's not skinny. Her coat is in good shape. Her eyes are bright. She must belong to someone." Wanda rubbed her cheek against the cat's softness. "I'll put an ad in the Lost and Found section of the newspaper. Maybe we can find the owner that way."

"Do it today," Wishbone said. "Give the kitten to the first person who asks for her."

"And if no one claims her, maybe I'll keep her. She is sweet," Wanda said.

"Wanda, don't you know anything?" Wishbone said. "Cats are sneaky. You can't trust them."

"And you need a name," Wanda said, as she stroked the cat's thick coat.

"No! Don't give her a name!" Wishbone pleaded. "Don't do anything at all to make her seem the least bit permanent."

"I'll call you Pixie," Wanda said. "I've always wanted a pet."

"Cat's are *pests,* not *pets,*" Wishbone said. "And that one extra letter makes all the difference."

"Look at the way she's gazing at Wishbone!" Joe said. "I've never seen a cat stare at a dog like that before. It's almost as if she likes him."

"Don't say the "L" word unless you mean liver snaps! Oh, no," Wishbone said. "A kitten at Wanda's house will spell disaster." Already Wishbone could picture the scene—Pixie lolling on his favorite spot on Wanda's porch. Pixie landscaping Wanda's yard the way Wishbone liked to do himself. "I'll never be able to go over to Wanda's house now," Wishbone said.

"You must be hungry," Wanda crooned to the cat. "You poor little lost kitty. I'll bet you're hungry." As soon as they got to Wanda's house, she took Pixie inside with her and closed the door.

What an afternoon, Wishbone thought. He and Joe were planning on tailing Damont tomorrow. This afternoon, though, it seemed as if that kitten had been tailing him! But why? And how could Wishbone stop her? It seemed as if Wishbone had his own mystery to solve now, as well as the one he shared with Joe!

Chapter Eight

The next day, Wishbone got up bright and early. One of his most important responsibilities in the Talbot household was to get Joe ready for school and out the door. He knew an alarm clock was nothing compared to a dog's bark! He stood at the foot of Joe's bed and gave his buddy his best wake-up call.

Joe roused. "Oh, Wishbone," he said, muffling his voice in his pillow.

Wishbone barked again. "Come on, Joe, we have a lot to do today," Wishbone said.

He watched Joe get out of bed and wash and dress. Occasionally, he barked, to make sure Joe knew he didn't have a lot of time. When Joe was finally through washing up, he sat on the edge of his bed and grabbed for yesterday's socks. Wishbone leaped forward and tugged at them until Joe released his grip and got up. Joe went to the dresser for a fresh pair of socks. It didn't take Joe long to finish dressing and comb his hair.

"Breakfast," Joe announced to Wishbone.

"Ah, the benefits of my job." Wishbone sighed,

thinking of the day's first meal. He followed Joe downstairs to the kitchen. Joe always ate breakfast with Ellen. Wishbone waited until Joe had finished every bit of his toast and eggs. Then he gave his "you're going to be late" bark and nudged at Joe's leg.

Ellen laughed. "I think Wishbone's telling you to get going," she said.

"All right," Joe said. He got up and Wishbone barked again. Wishbone ran to the counter where Joe's lunch was waiting, all wrapped, and wagged his tail. "Almost forgot my lunch," Joe said. He went over to the counter and grabbed it. Then he bent down to pat Wishbone. "Thanks, Wishbone," he said.

"Just doing my job," Wishbone said proudly.

Joe grabbed his *Ten Little Indians* book. Ellen kissed him good-bye and then opened the door. "Want to go out, Wishbone?" she asked.

"Sure. Why not?" Wishbone said, and he sauntered outside into the fresh air. He sniffed all around. No cat seemed to be nearby. That was a good sign. He couldn't wait to start tailing Damont after school. Wishbone's tail was on full alert, positioned upright. His ears were perked nicely. His nose was on high-speed sniff duty.

What to do, what to do, in the meantime? Wishbone thought. There were cars to chase. That was always a good way to pass the time. There were yards to romp through. No choice that he came up with, though, felt quite right to him. He concentrated. . . . *Wait!* Wishbone thought. *What I really want to do is—try to help Joe out! Why can't I start my tailing without him?*

Wishbone put all his senses on red alert. *We dogs*

don't usually have to turn ourselves on full power at once, but this is an emergency. I have to help Joe. His ears perked up so he could catch any suspicious sound. His whiskers stood out, acting like radar to detect any sudden, strange movement. Best of all was his keen sense of smell. Lifting his nose, he could smell eggs frying in a pan three blocks away. He sniffed a bit harder. A familiar odor struck him. *Fur,* he thought. *Fish!* Oh, no, he hadn't escaped, after all! It was *the cat!*

What a disaster! Wishbone turned around, pretending to be nonchalant, and there was Pixie. "Scat!" he ordered. Pixie purred. *Great,* Wishbone thought. *If there's one thing a dog detective doesn't need, it's a loud purring sound calling attention to him.*

Wishbone started to trot down the street. He turned, and there was Pixie still following him. "Please go home," he begged, but Pixie continued to follow him. "Don't you know dog rules?" Wishbone said. "I chase. You run away. I bark. You run away. Want to practice?"

Wishbone tried to chase Pixie. He put on as ferocious a face as he could, running hard. Pixie looked startled for a moment and backed up. Wishbone kept running, sure that any moment she would start acting like a cat and get out of his way. He tried to look even meaner as he ran ever closer to her.

"Get out of the way!" he cried.

The kitten wouldn't budge. Finally, Wishbone had to veer off, tumbling into the grass. When he straightened himself up, Pixie was rolling in the dewy grass, happily meowing. It was a sound that made Wishbone think of nails scratching on a window.

"Sorry, but I don't speak your language," Wishbone told Pixie. "But I hope what you're saying is, 'So long, it's been nice knowing you, but now I have to be on my way.' "

Wishbone looked anxiously down the street.

"This will ruin my standing in dog society if any of my canine cousins sees a cat being friendly to me. And what if all the other cats decide they don't have to run if I chase them? Then I will be in really big trouble. Why, this could turn everything upside down in the dog world. There are certain rules to follow, you know." He barked at the cat, who purred even louder. "Can't you at least purr more softly? I can't hear myself think. And stop looking at me as if I were a plate of sardines!"

The kitten came closer to Wishbone.

"That's it," Wishbone said. "I'll just ignore you."

Wishbone decided to go for a long walk. He trotted toward the clubhouse at Jackson Park. He tried his best to lose Pixie by doing his doggiest things. Wishbone ran toward a fence, digging under it, just enough so he could squeeze through. He knew from experience that cats hated what he called affectionately "the big squeeze." Surely he'd lose Pixie now! Wishbone finished digging and balled himself as small as he could, pushing his way under the fence.

Puffing, he shook the dirt from his paws, and then he turned around, triumphant. But to his surprise, there was Pixie, delicately making her way under the fence. Wasn't that just like a cat, using the hole a dog had dug?

Pixie sat down and began to lick her paws leisurely. Wishbone sighed.

"Try to be quiet, at least," Wishbone told Pixie. "I

have work to do." He sniffed at the ground, trying to find something that didn't smell like the forest. He prowled around, trying to go wherever it was that Pixie wasn't. He sniffed at the air. He could tell by the scent that it was still early, and Joe wouldn't be out of school for hours. He continued his leisurely walk, until he finally found himself in Jackson Park.

Wishbone yawned. There was just so much investigation he could do on his own, especially when he was getting tired. He didn't need to be a detective to know the solution to that problem was to take a nap! And once he was dreaming, he wouldn't be aware of the kitten at all. Wishbone found a patch of grass in the sun and lay down. He yawned again, ignoring the kitten, and shut his eyes. Before he knew it, he was asleep in doggie dreamland.

By the time Wishbone woke up, it was three o'clock. Joe would be getting out of school right about then. Joe had said he was going to check out the clubhouse first, and Wishbone would be there waiting for him. He shook the sleep from his four legs and stared at the kitten, who was sleeping near him.

"Nice to see you, but now it's time for me to go," Wishbone said.

He ran as fast as he could to the clubhouse, and sure enough, not more than a few minutes went by until Joe showed up on his bike.

Joe checked around the outside of the clubhouse. He didn't want to spend a long time there. He just wanted to do a quick check to see if he could uncover any clues to help him figure out the mysterious events that were occurring. Then he and Wishbone would tail Damont around town. Damont should be easy to find. He had his usual hangouts. He liked pizza, so he might drop by Pepper Pete's Pizza Parlor. He also liked to spend time shooting hoops by the school.

Joe studied the clubhouse. It seemed to be in good shape. Sam had told him earlier at school that her father was going to bring some furniture over for them to use. Joe saw that Mr. Kepler had dropped off a small blue bookshelf, and a blue card table with three chairs. He had even brought a small red rag rug for the kids to place in the center of the floor to make the clubhouse more homey. And they had plans for it to look even better. Joe trailed his hand along the bare windows. Maybe some curtains would be nice.

Joe scanned the clubhouse. He wasn't sure what he was looking for. He had a feeling he would know as soon as he saw it. He couldn't help but feel more and more excited that he would surely soon find the answer to this mystery—and it wouldn't involve a ghost! He walked around the clubhouse and then crouched down in the grass nearby and ran his fingers through it. All that happened was that a grasshopper flew by.

Joe heard Wishbone bark, and he stood up. He looked at Wishbone, and for a second he thought he saw something move behind the dog. Joe shook his head. But then he saw that "something" move again, and it came into sudden focus. "It's a cat!" Joe said.

Pixie the cat! He laughed. The cat was standing next to Wishbone, and Wishbone didn't look too happy about it. "Never mind, Wishbone," Joe said. "You can help me over here. Come on, maybe you can dig up some clues with me."

Joe still wasn't quite sure what to look for. He stepped inside the clubhouse and looked around. He ran his hands along the walls. Then he lifted up the table and chairs, then set them down again. He checked in all the corners. He went around to all the windows, opening and closing them. Finally, he stood in the center of the clubhouse, wondering what to do next. Suddenly, he heard something rustling. He couldn't tell where the sound came from. Joe tried to tell himself it was probably nothing. He listened harder, to pinpoint the sound, but this time all he heard was Wishbone, barking excitedly outside.

Joe went back outside. Wishbone was in the bushes with Pixie, tugging something away from her. "This is no time to play," Joe said.

He walked over to the bushes to separate the two. There was Wishbone with a small portable tape recorder held firmly in his mouth!

"What's this doing here?" Joe asked.

He took it away from Wishbone's firm grasp and pressed down on the Play button. Suddenly a voice boomed, *"Get Out!"*

Pixie leaped back, hissing, her back arched, her whiskers spread out. Joe felt electrified. This was it! This was the clue he had been looking for—the solid proof! A human being had set up this stunt, not a ghost! But was it Damont?

Joe held the tape recorder closer to his ear. Whose voice was that? It didn't sound like Damont's. But it did sound familiar. Was this Damont's tape recorder? Wishbone sniffed at it. Joe turned it over in his hands. He was nearly bursting with excitement. Now he really wanted to tail Damont, but he decided to wait for his other friends to show up first, so he could show them this incredible new clue.

Chapter Nine

Now Joe couldn't wait for the rest of the gang to arrive. He went back inside the clubhouse and sat down at the card table with the tape recorder. Wishbone and Pixie followed him in. He kept playing the message over and over, trying to identify the voice. Every time Joe played it, Wishbone barked and Pixie hissed. The voice was low and very slow, almost as if someone had deliberately used a fake voice to disguise their own. The "out" sounded as if it were two words—*ow-ut!* Joe was listening to the tape for the tenth time in a row when his friends showed up.

Sam saw Joe was holding a tape recorder when she and the others came into the clubhouse. "What's that for?" she asked. She sat down on a chair.

The other kids crowded around Joe. Bobby was startled when he saw the tape recorder. "That's my tape recorder!" he exclaimed. Joe stared at him in surprise. Bobby took the recorder from Joe, turning it over in his hands. "I thought I lost this!" he said.

Joe narrowed his eyes. "*You* lost it?" he said.

Bobby nodded. "I lost it last week. But what's it doing here?"

Henrietta tried to reach for the recorder. "I told you it would turn up," she said. "I told you I didn't take it."

Sam studied Bobby. "Why does it have dirt all over it? Did you dig that up, Wishbone?"

"Wait a minute, wait a minute!" Joe said. He reached to press the Play button on the tape recorder, all the while keeping his eyes glued on Bobby's face to see his reaction.

"Get out!" boomed the voice.

Startled, Bobby's mouth flew open. He tried to grab the tape recorder from Joe, and it fell on the floor. Joe moved back.

"What is going on here?" Joe asked.

Henrietta stared at Bobby.

"Is this a joke, Bobby?" David asked quietly.

Bobby frowned. "What are you talking about! How can you accuse me?" he said. "Someone else must have recorded that message! It wasn't me. But who? And how did they get the recorder from me to bring it here?"

Bobby looked and acted so genuinely surprised that Joe felt even more confused. If the "ghost" wasn't Bobby, then who was it?

"Where did you have the tape recorder last?" Joe asked.

Bobby grew thoughtful. "Well, I took it to school for a project in my journalism class. I was going to interview another student. I wanted to tape the interview the way real journalists do. I put it in my knapsack. I didn't look in my knapsack again until after dinner that day. Then I saw it was gone. I couldn't figure out where it was."

"Who else was in that class?" Joe asked.

Bobby's face suddenly lightened. "Damont was in that class! He could have taken the recorder and made up that voice."

Joe nodded vigorously. "Come on, Wishbone. Let's go try to find him now."

Just then there was the same soft rustling sound Joe had heard before! He hushed everyone and listened carefully, trying to figure out where the sound was coming from. Sam looked around, and Bobby frowned so deeply that he made big "worry" lines stretch across his forehead. Henrietta gripped the edge of the table, her knuckles turning white. Joe stood up, pushing back his chair. He listened again. There it was. The rustling was coming from one of the side walls, right near the bookshelf. Wishbone started to sniff and wag his tail fiercely. Pixie began to move slowly toward the wall, her eyes alert, her tail twitching.

The soft rustling sound continued. Wishbone ran over to the shelf and began to paw at it.

"Is it a ghost?" Sam asked.

Joe gathered his courage, not wanting anyone to think he was afraid. He strode over to the shelf and took in a deep breath. He didn't know what he expected to find. Crouching down, he moved the shelf, just a bit. Suddenly, something flew out at him!

Joe toppled over backward, stunned. He looked up. This was no ghost! A tiny gray baby bird flew up in the air and then fell back down. Pixie ran toward the

bird, but not before Wishbone could run interference and keep her away.

Bobby raced over, bending down, about to cup the bird in his hands, when Henrietta cried out, "No! Don't do that!"

Bobby was startled by her loud voice. The other kids looked at her in amazement.

Henrietta's face flushed red. She took a step back. When she spoke again, her voice was soft. "If you get your human scent on her, her mother won't come and get her," Henrietta said. "It probably just fell out of the nest and got lost and somehow came in here."

Bobby looked at Henrietta in surprise. Then he glanced at the bird. It seemed to be terrified. Sam and David both came over, too, and they bent down to check it out. Wishbone barked and then ran outside, chasing Pixie. When Pixie had disappeared from sight, Wishbone began pawing at the ground.

"We need to feed it worms," Henrietta said.

Bobby held up one finger and then moved toward the door. "I'll take care of it," he said. He rushed outside. In minutes, he was back, carrying something in his hand. He crouched down and dangled a fat worm, carefully placing it right near the tiny bird's beak.

Henrietta shook her head. "It can't eat a whole worm!" Henrietta said, kneeling down near the bird. "That's something you see only in cartoons. You have to mash it up, the way the mother would do."

Joe looked at Henrietta with new respect. How did she know all that? Then he glanced over at Bobby, who was shaking his head with admiration. Bobby put one hand on his sister's shoulder. "I never realized you knew so much about birds," he said.

Henrietta blushed, pleased by the compliment. She stood up. "This worm is dead. I'll mash the worm with my shoe and feed it to her with the tweezers we keep in the first-aid kit I brought. We should put her outside so her mom can see her easily." Henrietta bent down and carefully and slowly moved her hands toward the bird. She never once touched it, but her hands came close enough so that she was able to guide the bird slowly toward the door. Henrietta kept shooing the bird gently until it was finally outside, safe under a leafy tree. The other kids came outside to watch what Henrietta was doing. Next, she took the worm and mashed it with her shoe. She gently fed it to the bird by placing it on the tip of the tweezers. She was careful not to let her fingers touch the bird.

Joe felt a little undecided. On the one hand, he wanted to stay there with everyone else and watch Henrietta care for the baby bird. But he and Wishbone had an important mission to accomplish. They had to go tail Damont. Joe clapped his hands for Wishbone.

"We'll be back soon," Joe told the other kids. "We're going to go tail Damont. We'll see you in a little while." Joe got on his bike and began to pedal out of the park, as Wishbone followed behind.

Sam, David, and Bobby huddled closer around Henrietta, watching her in fascination. They didn't seem to see Joe and Wishbone leave.

Wishbone trotted excitedly after Joe. He didn't mind leaving the baby bird because he knew it was being taken care of nicely by Henrietta. Dogs could always tell which people were going to be good to them, and Wishbone guessed that birds must have that sense, too. Wishbone was ready to tail Damont!

"Tailing is in my genes, not to mention at the end of my body," Wishbone said. "I'm a hunter of table scraps, a sniffer of clues!"

Joe and Wishbone made their way to the center of Oakdale. Joe got off his bike, locked it up, and walked down the main street. "Damont usually stops at Pepper Pete's for a slice after school," Joe said. "Sometimes he's there for hours. I bet we can find him there."

"And we can get some pizza while we're at it, too," Wishbone suggested.

They headed for Pepper Pete's. "Let's keep a low

profile, Wishbone," Joe said. "We don't want to attract any attention to ourselves."

Wishbone slunk down along the ground. "Is this low enough for you, Joe?" he asked. "Secret Agent Dog, that's me."

"There he is," Joe whispered. "Look."

Damont was coming out of Pepper Pete's, chewing on a wedge of pizza. Tall and thin, he was wearing a T-shirt with a design of a basketball hoop on it, and he was sporting dark sunglasses.

"That pizza looks very suspicious to me," Wishbone said. "I say we grab it as evidence."

"Let's follow him," Joe said.

Damont crossed the street and began to walk down Main Street, past Rosie's Rendezvous Books & Gifts. He stopped once, and Joe quickly turned to look in a window of Beck's Grocery. When Joe peered around again, all Damont was doing was bending over and tying his shoelace.

"We'll catch him soon," Joe said, "now that we know it's a real person doing the haunting. Boy, superstition can really shake you up. In *Ten Little Indians,* all the guests are positive that a mysterious host is killing them off. I read a little bit more in school today, and I got to the part where the guests become brave enough to search the island. They discover there is no one else on it but them. Now they're looking at one another, trying to see who's acting suspiciously. Why can't Damont do something like that right now?" Joe asked.

"I'm always suspicious of a boy who doesn't share his pizza," Wishbone said.

When Damont started to walk again, Joe and Wishbone followed, keeping their heads down.

"Act casual," Wishbone said. "Act as if this is nothing more than a late-afternoon stroll."

Just then Damont stopped abruptly.

"Joe! Wishbone!" a voice called.

Joe looked up. There, not too far away from Damont, stood Wanda. Damont turned around and gave Joe and Wishbone a surprised look.

"Hi, Damont," Wanda said. "Isn't it a lovely day?"

Damont started walking toward Wanda. He waited for Joe and Wishbone to catch up. Soon all four were standing in a circle on the sidewalk.

"Perfect for taking a nice long walk," Joe said.

"Come up with a better excuse, Joe," Wishbone urged his buddy. "Say that we were on our way to the track for a run."

"Hello, Ms. Gilmore," Damont said with a smile on his face.

"Did you ever find out who or what is haunting the clubhouse?" Wanda asked.

Damont grinned. "The clubhouse is haunted?" he said. "Boy, if there's one thing I hate, it's haunted clubhouses. I'm sure glad I wasn't the one who won it. But if I did, you can bet I'd be smart enough to catch the ghost."

"It's not haunted," Joe insisted. "We found a tape recorder with a voice on it saying *'Get out!'* A real person did that, not any ghost." Wishbone noticed how hard Joe was studying Damont.

"Whoever is doing the haunting must be pretty clever," Damont said. "I'd say really, really clever."

86

Suddenly, Damont sneezed—again and again, as if he were allergic to something.

Wishbone sniffed the air. "What's that funny smell?" he asked. "Wanda, did something go bad in your purse?"

Damont sneezed again.

"I hope it's not my perfume," Wanda said. "I found a formula for it in a book, and I made it up myself—right on the kitchen stove. Hibiscus flowers and rose petals are the main ingredients. I call it Joy of Wanda. Do you like it?"

Damont sneezed again.

"It's very nice," Joe said doubtfully.

"Personally, my favorite perfume is hamburger," Wishbone said.

Damont sneezed, covering his nose and mouth with his hands. "I'd better go."

"It must be the flu that's going around," Wanda said.

Damont walked away from them, turning the nearest corner. Even after Wishbone couldn't see him, he could still hear Damont sneezing.

"I still think he's our prime suspect," Joe said. "He was last seen near the tape recorder."

"Innocent until proven guilty," Wanda said, raising one finger.

"Well, we just need solid proof," Joe said. "But what?" Joe stroked Wishbone's head, just the way he liked. "Let's grab my bike and head back to the club-house," he said. "Maybe one of the other kids will have some ideas."

Chapter Ten

The entire time Joe was biking back to the clubhouse, he couldn't stop plotting how to catch Damont. He'd have to tail him some more. Maybe he'd have to go to his house and look for clues—but *what* clues? And how in the world would he ever get invited into Damont's house? At least in *Ten Little Indians,* all the people were together on one island, in one house, and they couldn't really hide anywhere. This case was going to be much more difficult.

When Joe and Wishbone got back to the clubhouse, the door was closed. *They must be inside,* Joe thought. Then he saw a white piece of paper tacked up on the front door. Maybe the other kids had all gone home and left him this note. He went over and took it down. Typed in the center of the page, in capital letters, was the warning: GET OUT!

Get out? Joe felt a shiver of ice run up his spine. Wishbone barked, and the door to the clubhouse opened. Sam grinned at him. "What's that?" she said.

Joe handed her the paper. Her face seemed to go

white. The other kids stood up and came toward Joe and Sam, crowding around the note.

"I didn't see or hear anyone come near the clubhouse, let alone tack up a note," Sam said. Bobby shook his head as if to say, me neither.

"I went back outside before to check on the bird," Henrietta said. "I didn't see anyone."

"I was so *sure* our 'ghost' was Damont," Joe said. "But could Damont have had time to make up that note and leave it here?" Joe said. "Wishbone and I were tailing him all this time."

"Who else could it be, then?" Henrietta asked.

David studied the note. He pointed a finger excitedly at the piece of paper. "Look at this!" he said. "There's a broken piece on both of the *T*'s."

"So?" said Sam.

"So, the note must have been typed on an old typewriter, or one with a broken key. I think all we have to do is find a typewriter with a broken *T*, and then we'll have found the person who typed this note. We will have discovered our ghost!"

"How are we going to do that?" Henrietta asked.

"By a process of deduction," Joe said. "Who do we know who uses a typewriter?"

"Don't look at me. I have a computer," David said. "So do a lot of other people nowadays."

Joe tried to think. His mother had a computer. There was no typewriter store in Oakdale, but the library had a few typewriters. That was it!

"Let's go check out the library!" Joe said. "There are a couple of typewriters there. Maybe one of them has a broken *T* key!"

The kids grabbed their bikes. They pedaled through the park and headed off toward the library. Wishbone ran alongside. The closer they got to the Oakdale Public Library, the more excited Joe became. He knew they'd find something, he just knew it! He really felt like a detective now.

They parked their bikes outside the library. Joe bent and petted Wishbone. "You have to stay here for a little while," he said. Wishbone's tail visibly drooped. "I know you're disappointed, but this shouldn't take very long."

Joe and the other kids climbed the steps two at a time and then entered the library. The typewriters were in a back room in the basement of the library, where someone typing wouldn't disturb anyone. Joe and the others raced down the stairs, panting. One person was typing; it was a boy who looked to be a few years older than any one of them. But the other typewriters were not being used. Joe motioned to Sam to check out the typewriter by the far wall. Bobby, Henrietta, and David started to examine the typewriters by the windows. Joe pointed at the boy who was typing. He'd check out that typewriter himself.

Joe quietly approached the boy, leaning over behind him, trying to see if all the keys worked properly. He thought that he was being really quiet, but the boy suddenly turned around and scowled at Joe.

"I'm trying to concentrate," he said.

Joe leaned forward. "Does the *T* on your type-writer work okay?" he blurted out.

The boy gave him a quizzical look. "I wouldn't be typing on this machine if it didn't." He pointed to the page he was typing, showing Joe a perfect letter *T*. Joe's heart sank.

He looked over at Sam, who was busy checking out the other typewriter. She finally stood up and shook her head. Bobby turned from the typewriter he was at to face them, shaking his head. Then David did the same thing, too.

"Now what do we do?" Sam asked.

Joe didn't know what to do next. He wasn't aware of any other public place in Oakdale that had type-writers. If someone had one in his or her home, there wasn't any way for him to find it. He pushed a hand through his hair, completely frustrated at coming up empty. This detective work was a lot harder than he had expected.

Sam looked at her watch. "Well, I'm going home. I'll try to think of something tonight. Maybe we can just start watching in school for people who type their homework and check for broken letters or something."

"I don't feel like going home just yet. I'm going to walk a little with Wishbone," Joe said.

The whole group left the library and walked down the steps out front. Joe waved good-bye to the other kids and set off. He was walking his bike down the street with Wishbone at his side when he passed the Oakdale Attic Antiques store. He had bought his mom a wonderful music box there for Mother's Day two years ago. Joe peered in one of the windows.

Suddenly, he had a terrific thought. Typewriters were practically antique. Maybe Mr. Johnson, the owner, would know something that could help. "Come on, Wishbone, you're allowed to come in here, too," Joe said.

Oakdale Attic Antiques had a big, friendly looking white entrance door. On either side of it was decorative brickwork, and the windowpanes were painted a warm shade of red. There was always some kind of interesting display in the windows. The bell attached to the door rang cheerfully when Joe walked in. The store was quiet and pleasant and filled with wonderful, unusual items. There were glass lamps and old rocking chairs and a wicker bird cage. Joe ran his hand along a highly polished, carved wood table. There was a large glass curio cabinet over near the cash register. Inside it were all sorts of antique jewelry and hand-painted boxes.

Just then Mr. Johnson came out from behind a curtained partition at the back of the shop. He was a big man with a full head of curly hair. His eyes were twinkling from behind his glasses. He always wore sweaters, so he looked really comfortable.

"Oh, Joe," he said. "What can I help you with?"

Joe looked around the shop and was about to ask Mr. Johnson what he knew about typewriters when he spotted one in a corner. His heart leaped. Maybe—just maybe—this was the one.

"Do you mind if I try out that typewriter?" Joe asked.

"Sure, go ahead. It's a real beauty. There's paper already in her," said Mr. Johnson.

Joe walked over, his heart beating rapidly. He typed "OUT THE DOOR," squinting down at the page. The *T* was perfect—absolutely no sign of a break in the letter! His face fell.

"No good?" Mr. Johnson said. "Wrong color?" He smiled. "I have another machine, in the back, but I have to fix it. I didn't even notice anything was wrong with it until a little girl came in and was playing with it and I saw that the *T* was broken."

Joe straightened. "The *T* was broken?" Wishbone let loose with one quick, loud bark, as if he were showing Joe that he, too, found this new bit of information very interesting, indeed.

"That's what I said. It should be fixed tomorrow, if you're interested in trying it out," Mr. Johnson said. "That little girl sure had her eye on it."

"The little girl?" Joe asked.

Mr. Johnson nodded. "Cute as a button. Red hair.

Blue eyes. Lots of freckles. I haven't seen her around here before, and I pride myself on knowing most of the people in Oakdale."

Joe motioned to Wishbone. His mind was swirling in circles. This girl sounded a lot like Henrietta, but why would she ever do such a thing as to write that threatening note?

Chapter Eleven

All the way home, Joe couldn't stop thinking about Henrietta. Why would she make the clubhouse seem to be haunted? In the mystery he was reading, *Ten Little Indians*, the ten guests on the island were certain that the killer was actually one of them. But which one? Each one of them had something dark in his or her past that made them possible suspects. But that still didn't answer the question of *"why?"*

Joe was sure that Henrietta was guilty. But someone couldn't just be accused out of thin air. There had to be evidence that proved beyond a doubt that she was responsible—like fingerprints. He couldn't get those. And even if she had been using that typewriter, did that still really prove that she had tacked up the note on the clubhouse door? She would have to confess! But how could Joe get her to do that?

Wishbone licked Joe's hand. "It's okay, Wishbone, I'm just trying to figure something out," Joe said to him. Tomorrow, he would have to go right to her house after school let out, instead of going directly to the clubhouse. He'd confront her on his own. Then he would decide what to do next.

The next day at school passed slowly. Joe told Sam that he'd be late in arriving at the clubhouse, that he had to do some chore for his mom. Joe couldn't stop thinking about Henrietta being the "ghost." He never would have suspected her! He was so sure it had been Damont, but Damont couldn't have posted the note at the very same time Joe had been tailing him in the center of town. And Damont wasn't even in school today. Joe heard a teacher say Damont had the flu.

Finally, the last bell rang, signaling the end of the day's classes. Joe raced out of the school. Wishbone was dutifully waiting for his pal out near the sidewalk. Henrietta's house was only a few blocks away.

Joe stood outside Henrietta's house with Wishbone, waiting for her to come home. Joe glanced all around, trying to catch sight of Henrietta.

Suddenly, there she was! She came walking down the street alone. She clutched her books up against her chest. Her head was down. Watching her, Joe felt a twinge deep in his stomach. His heart went out to her because she looked so sad.

Behind Henrietta was another little girl who seemed to be around her own age. She was also walking alone. This little girl had short blond curly hair and wore a red dress. Even though she walked straight and held her head high, she looked a little lonely to Joe, too. Henrietta didn't seem to notice her, though.

"Henrietta!" Joe called. Wishbone barked a greeting. The little redhead looked up and grinned.

She walked over and bent to pet Wishbone, who wagged his tail happily. "What are you guys doing here?" she asked. "I was on my way over to the clubhouse to see if the mother bird had come back for her lost baby."

"Oh, I just wanted to talk to you about something," Joe said. Henrietta rubbed Wishbone behind his ears, one of his favorite places for a quick massage. She didn't look directly into Joe's eyes.

Just at that moment the other little girl approached. Wishbone suddenly raced around and around her, so fast that she had to stop, right in front of Henrietta's house. The little girl stood still, looking astonished. She finally glanced over at Henrietta. "Is that your dog?" she asked Henrietta.

Henrietta looked up and shook her head. "This is Wishbone. He's Joe's dog."

The other girl nodded. "Well, he sure wanted me to stop."

Henrietta looked worried.

"I like dogs a lot," the girl said.

"Me, too," said Henrietta. "I know a lot about them."

"You do?" said the girl. "Maybe you could help me out. I'm thinking of getting a dog. Maybe you could tell me which kinds make the best pets."

Henrietta brightened. "Sure."

The other girl hesitated. "Well, I had better go home," she said reluctantly. She turned and started to walk away. Then she suddenly stopped. Turning toward Henrietta, she gave a shy smile. "My name is Milly," she said.

"I'm Henrietta."

"Maybe I'll see you again tomorrow, Henrietta," said Milly.

Henrietta and Joe watched Milly as she walked away. Suddenly, Joe noticed that Henrietta seemed full of energy. She stood up straighter. Joe knew why. She had finally befriended someone her own age. He was happy for her, but he put that thought aside. They had something to discuss.

"Let's take a walk," Joe said.

Henrietta looked doubtful, but she walked with Joe and Wishbone. Eventually, they came to a bench shaded by a large tree, and the two sat down. Wishbone sat at Henrietta's feet, putting a paw on one of her sneakers, as if to comfort her.

Henrietta still couldn't look directly at Joe. She kept her head down.

"I went to the Oakdale Attic Antiques shop yesterday," Joe said.

Henrietta thrust her head down even farther. She began petting Wishbone. She wouldn't even look in Joe's direction.

"I tried out a typewriter there to see if it might have been the one used to make the note we found on the clubhouse door, but the *T* was perfect," Joe said.

Henrietta kept stroking Wishbone, ruffling his fur.

"Then Mr. Johnson, the owner, told me about another typewriter he was fixing in the back of the shop." Joe paused. "That one had a broken *T*."

"Oh!" Henrietta said, her voice cracking. "You found the typewriter that was used to make the note! That's great!"

"Henrietta," Joe said, "Mr. Johnson told me a little girl was playing around with it the other day. He said the girl had red hair, blue eyes, and freckles."

Henrietta stopped petting Wishbone. She sat up straight and suddenly looked right at Joe. Her voice was so full of misery that Joe didn't know what to do.

"I thought you'd kick me out of your club," she said sadly.

Joe shook his head. "Why did you think that?"

"Bobby told me over and over that I didn't belong with older kids. I saw how you all liked him and how you were his friend. I thought he'd convince all of you that I didn't belong in the club and you would all want me to leave, too. It made me upset. I thought that if I wasn't going to be allowed in the club, then neither could anyone else."

Joe studied Henrietta. He couldn't believe she was the one responsible for all the hauntings. "We wouldn't have kicked you out," Joe said. "I think Bobby was just hoping you'd find friends your own age."

Henrietta hung her head with shame. "I took Bobby's tape recorder and recorded that scary voice. I typed the note, too. When everyone thought I was just checking up on the baby bird, I was attaching the note to the door of the clubhouse." Henrietta folded her hands in a tight knot. "I did something terrible, didn't I?" Then she swiped at her eyes as if she were going to cry. "Now you'll really kick me out."

Joe shook his head slowly. "No, we won't," he said. "I know you don't believe me, but I'll bet anything that one day you won't want to hang around with us older kids."

"Are you going to tell on me?" Henrietta asked.

Joe was silent for a moment. "Are you going to stop haunting the clubhouse?"

Henrietta nodded vigorously. "I promise." She hesitated. "I didn't make that face appear in the picture, you know. I don't know *what* that was. I just got the idea to do what I did from that."

"It was probably nothing," Joe said.

Joe was thoughtful. If he didn't tell the others about Henrietta's prank, they would never know who had haunted the clubhouse. But if he did tell, Bobby would probably insist that she not come to the clubhouse anymore. The truth of the matter was that now

Joe felt a great sense of relief. There was no ghost. There had been only a lonely little girl who had wanted to feel she belonged to a group.

"Okay, Henrietta," Joe said. "Since you've been honest with me, this entire matter will stay between you and me."

So, the mystery was finally solved. Joe and Henrietta biked over to the clubhouse. Wishbone trotted happily alongside his companions. The other kids' bikes were already parked outside on the grass.

"Look!" Henrietta cried, pointing to the big tree nearby. "The baby bird is gone. Her mom must have come back for her." She was so happy she giggled.

"Thanks to you," Joe said, making Henrietta smile more. "Come on," Joe said. "Let's go inside."

In the clubhouse, Sam and David were sitting at the card table. Bobby stood nearby as they talked about how to find the ghost. A big package of pretzels laid open at the center of the table, and everyone was munching handfuls. Bobby was layering his pretzels one on top of another, as if he were building some kind of a structure.

Henrietta bounded toward the table. "The baby bird's mother took her home!" she said excitedly.

Bobby leaned over and ruffled Henrietta's hair. "Know anything about getting a ghost to leave here, Henrietta?" Bobby asked.

Henrietta's good mood disappeared, and she looked down at the floor.

"I bet it will just stop bothering us," Joe said quickly. "I bet whoever is pulling these pranks will just get bored and stop." Sam looked doubtful.

"Why should it stop?" Sam asked. She grew thoughtful and then brightened suddenly.

Joe recognized that look. Sam was getting an idea and he wasn't sure how he was going to feel about it.

"I know!" Sam said excitedly. "Ghosts always come out after dark. What if we stay late tonight—say, until ten? I'll prove there isn't a ghost by catching whoever is doing this. Who agrees with me?"

They all nodded in agreement.

Sam's eyes twinkled with excitement. "Let's do it tonight. We can ride our bikes home and tell our parents, and then we'll come right back here."

"I can't stay," David said. "My aunt's coming over later and I have to be home. I don't feel so well, anyway. It must be the flu that's going around. A lot of kids have been coming down with it. Even Damont was out sick today. I heard a teacher say Damont has it really bad. I hope I can fight it off."

"You take care of yourself. I can stay here. Sam, stop by my house, tell my mom where I am, and pick up some stuff for me and Wishbone," Joe said. Wishbone nudged him. "Wishbone will keep me company while the rest of you are gone." He felt a little guilty. He knew that the only "ghost" haunting the clubhouse had been Henrietta, but he had promised her not to tell. Well, staying after dark in the clubhouse would prove to everyone else that there was no ghost. And the kids would have a lot of fun just by hanging out together.

"Good," Sam said. "We'll stop this ghost thing right in its tracks."

Chapter Twelve

Later that night, Wishbone sat with Joe, Bobby, Sam, and Henrietta on the floor of the clubhouse. His tail wagged happily because he was with his friends. Everyone had gone home and come back in record time. They each had brought back something for the long night ahead. Joe had his backpack with his copy of *Ten Little Indians* and a portable reading light. Wishbone had his favorite red-rubber chew bone and was giving it a taste test. Bobby had brought meatloaf sandwiches for everyone, plus two big Thermoses of hot chocolate, which he was carefully pouring into heat-proof cups. Sam came with a flashlight.

It was warm and comfortable in the clubhouse. Wishbone wasn't frightened at all. The only noises he heard were the whispering of the night breezes and the steady breathing of all the kids. Wishbone saw, though, that Sam and Bobby were nervous. He could sniff that scent of concern a mile away. Sam looked at the windows anxiously. Bobby got up to check the door. He opened it and peered outside.

Then he carefully shut it again. The only ones who were completely calm were Joe and Henrietta. They shared a secret. As far as they were concerned, there was no ghost.

Wishbone, though, wasn't so sure this particular mystery was completely solved. He gave his toy a thoughtful chew. He knew that dogs sometimes picked up on things that people couldn't sense. Dogs felt the truth deep in their bones, like a special tingling feeling. Now, he was not sure the haunting was over. There still might be a ghost, Wishbone thought, and it might be up to him to find it. Wishbone got up from where he had been resting and moved over to snuggle beside Joe. "Mind if I join you, Joe?" he asked. He settled himself down next to Joe.

Joe sighed contentedly. "This is kind of nice," he said. "But I still can't wait until the clubhouse is right in my backyard."

"Me, either, Joe," Wishbone said.

Just then, the door rattled, making Bobby jump. Sam stood up uncertainly. "It was just the wind," Sam said, trying to reassure herself.

"Sure, the wind," Bobby said.

Henrietta stood up, her face suddenly white. Joe put one hand on her shoulder, as if to steady her.

What's going on? Wishbone thought. *You don't think there is a ghost, because you were the ghost. Why are you acting as if there's a ghost now?*

Henrietta's hands were shaking. She pointed to the far window. "Look—" she whispered. A dim light flickered from outside. Then, suddenly, a shadowy figure moved past the window and disappeared!

"That is *not* the wind," Sam whispered. She wrapped both of her arms around herself.

The clubhouse suddenly felt cold. Wishbone sniffed at the air. But, try as he might, he couldn't smell anything but the heavenly aroma of the hot chocolate.

"Does the wind look like this?" Bobby gasped. He stared at one of the back windows. Speechless, he lifted his hand. Everyone looked at where he was pointing. A dim light flickered and then went out.

"Look!" Sam whispered.

There was the same strange shadowy figure. It was impossible to see anything but the eyes and nose and mouth. Wishbone watched as the figure took a few steps and then disappeared.

"That's not the wind," Sam whispered. "That looks like the same face that showed up in the first photograph we took. It looks like the face I saw in the wood patterns."

"It's probably nothing," Joe insisted, jumping up.

"A trick of light or something." He paced from one end of the cabin to the other. He stared out the window where the figure had passed by. "I don't see anyone outside—or *anything*."

"Don't worry, Joe. Secret Agent Dog is here," Wishbone said. "I'll protect you, no matter what's trying to spook us!"

Bobby suddenly wrapped his arms around himself. "It feels funny in here," Bobby said. "Colder and colder."

Then Henrietta started to feel cold, and she wrapped her arms around herself, too.

Sam rubbed her own arms. "It is getting chilly. And look how dark the sky is becoming. It looks as if it's going to rain."

"Rain—that's right," Joe said. "A natural phenomenon."

Wishbone felt something along the back of his fur. It didn't feel like the kind of prickling he felt when it was going to rain. Wishbone let out one strong, sharp bark. No, something else was going on, too—something he wasn't sure he was going to like. He barked again, trying to signal to Joe.

Joe bent and scratched Wishbone behind his left ear. "It's just a little rain," Joe reassured him.

Wishbone continued to bark. "Listen to me, Joe," he said. "Something's not right."

As if on cue, the rain began pouring down, drumming against the pine clubhouse. Joe suddenly relaxed. "I knew it was just the rain making things colder," Joe said. "I guess we're stuck here for a while."

"I don't know, but the rain makes me feel safer somehow," Sam said.

"Want to play cards?" Joe said. "I challenge you all to Crazy Eights."

"I'll get the deck," Bobby said.

Wishbone still felt a little rattled. He looked around the clubhouse. No strange shadows. No creepy sounds. Joe, Sam, and Bobby sat around the card table. "I'll deal," said Sam, flipping the cards.

Wishbone sat down behind Joe's chair. "Let me know when you need me," he said. He was watching Sam deal, when suddenly he felt something. He looked down. "Hey, my paws are wet," he said. He stood up, flicking water from his paws. "Not exactly drip-dry, are they?" he said. The floor was getting wetter and wetter. "Joe!" Wishbone barked. "Look out below!"

"Wishbone, hush! I have to check out my cards," Joe said.

But Wishbone kept barking, louder and louder, until Joe finally looked down. His sneakers were damp from the water, which was rising higher and higher even as he looked at it!

"The clubhouse is flooding!" Joe cried.

Chapter Thirteen

Wishbone barked as loud as he could. "Sound the alarm! Abandon clubhouse!" he called.

Joe looked down at the puddles forming on the floor. "Oh, no, the creek's probably overflowing, and we're in a low-lying area!"

"Let's get out of here!" Sam said. "I fold my hand!" She slammed the cards down on the table.

Joe went to the front door and tugged, but nothing happened. "It won't open!" Joe cried.

"It must just be jammed," Sam insisted. "Here, let me try." She spit on her hands and then rubbed them together. Next, she stood in front of the door and tugged at it, but it still wouldn't budge.

Henrietta looked as if she were going to cry. "I'm scared!" she said, lifting up her feet as the water was spreading across the clubhouse floor.

"I can't open it!" Sam shouted. She raised her feet one at a time, trying to prevent her sneakers from getting soaked. The water had risen to a depth of one inch. "And the water's getting higher!" Sam's sneakers began to feel soggy and waterlogged.

"I can't swim!" Bobby blurted out.

"Dog-paddle," Wishbone called out. "Just move your hands as if you're digging for a bone. That's how I learned."

Joe pushed again against the door with all his might, but it wouldn't budge. The water had now spread completely across the clubhouse floor. It was up to their ankles!

Wishbone jumped up on the table. "I'm all for heading to higher ground," he said. "Come on, there's room for more up here."

Sam looked around frantically. Her gaze finally settled on the three tiny windows in the clubhouse. "Try the windows," Sam called. "They're not big enough for us, but I bet Wishbone could crawl through and go get help. Bobby, you push the card table over to the window so Wishbone can jump up on it, while I get the window opened."

Joe ran over to one of the windows first and he tried to get it open. But it wouldn't even budge! "It's stuck!" Joe shouted. He tugged at the window again, but it was completely jammed shut.

Sam couldn't open one of the other two windows. Bobby ran to the third window and tugged at it with all his might. His face got red from the effort. He gave one last tug, which didn't budge the window, but it did send him sprawling down onto the floor and smack into the water. Soaking wet, he struggled back up and wiped the water from his face with his hands.

Bobby was really starting to panic. "This is getting very creepy," Bobby said. "These windows opened perfectly well yesterday! It's like someone is holding them down from outside!"

"Wishbone can't jump out of one of the windows and go for help if we can't get them open," Joe said.

"Someone or something—" Sam began to say.

"We have to try to do something—and fast!" Joe shouted.

"I want to go home!" Henrietta exclaimed. "I wish I had never set foot in this clubhouse! If I get out, I'll never come back here again."

Bobby wrapped his arms around Henrietta, giving her a hug. "I'll make sure that you get out safely," he promised.

Wishbone paced around nervously in circles on top of the table. "This is really serious," he said. "We're trapped. Good-bye to any more walks! Good-bye to chasing cars!"

"We're going to have to break one of the windows," Joe said with urgency. "Sam, can you hand me your flashlight?"

Sam looked around. The water was now above her ankles. "Where is it?" she cried.

"There it is!" Joe called. "Over there!"

Rolling back and forth in the water by the front door was the flashlight. Sam sloshed her way through the water to it. She crouched and picked up the flashlight. Then she made her way back to Joe and handed him the flashlight. He smashed it against one of the windows, taking care to cover his face. The glass shattered. He kept striking the glass, until he had knocked it all out of the window frame.

"Wishbone," Joe called. He stepped carefully

through the ever-rising water to the table, where Wishbone was standing, and picked him up.

"At your service," Wishbone said, panting. "I can do this, I know I can."

Joe lifted Wishbone up and then walked back to the open window frame. Wishbone was just able to manage to squeeze through the tiny window.

"Good thing I have such a trim figure," Wishbone said. He pushed off from the window with his hind legs. "Look out below!" Wishbone called. He jumped down, splashing into the water surrounding the clubhouse. Then he ran back toward the door. "No time to go for help. I've got to get the door open and rescue Joe and the others!" He pawed at the wood, then chewed at the door, but nothing happened.

"We can't just hang around here and wait," Bobby said. "I'll try the door one more time!" Bobby rammed his whole body against the door. Suddenly, as if by magic, it flew open! Bobby went sprawling onto the wet ground outside. He sputtered and kicked, then stood up.

"You got out!" Wishbone barked.

The rest of the kids ran outside onto the soggy ground.

"What is going on here?" Joe said.

Chapter Fourteen

Joe was cold and wet and totally confused. He slicked back his wet hair with one hand. He had thought the whole mystery had been solved when Henrietta had confessed to haunting the clubhouse. But then, tonight, something very unexpected and mysterious and scary had happened. Was there something going on at the clubhouse that *really* couldn't be explained? Had he been wrong about ghosts? Did they really exist? Were there some mysteries that just couldn't be solved?

Joe thought about his book *Ten Little Indians*. The characters in the story were still mysteriously dying, one by one. He had read up to the part where there were now only four characters left, and they were all very frightened. None of them knew what to do, either. Joe felt as if icy fingers were creeping up along his spine. He clapped his hands around his body for warmth. The rain kept pouring down over him. Joe noticed that Wishbone was sticking very close to him.

Joe stared at the clubhouse. Suddenly, he spotted

something that made him snap to attention. "Wait a minute!" he said. "Look at the windows!"

"What?" Sam said. She peered through the rain at the windows. Her hair was plastered to her scalp.

Joe walked over to the clubhouse. He ran his hands along the windows and then turned back to face the other kids. He smiled triumphantly, the rain running down his face. "These windows are nailed shut! Look at them. No ghost uses nails!" Joe cried.

The rain stopped abruptly. Sam, Bobby, and Henrietta looked up at the sky in amazement. They were all soaking wet. The ground was wet and very slippery. They all carefully made their way to the windows, hanging on to one another for support.

Sam took a careful look at the windows.

"They *are* all nailed shut!" Sam declared.

"What about the door? Why didn't it open?" Bobby asked.

Joe and Sam peered at the door.

Bobby quickly pulled on it, and it opened right up again. He ran his hands up and down along the wood. "I don't notice anything different about the door at all," he said. "It was as if someone put a tremendous amount of weight against it to keep us from getting out."

Just then there was the sound of footsteps.

"Who's there?" Joe shouted. He gazed out into the darkness. He could hear the footsteps coming closer and closer. His heart began to knock in his chest, louder and louder and louder.

A figure was coming toward them, closer and closer. Sam peered into the darkness. She shivered.

Joe stood tall. He stared out into the dark night

until he could see the face. "Wait a minute. It's—it's David!" he said with relief.

David sloshed across the soaked ground, and he was out of breath. He carried an umbrella.

"What are you doing here?" Bobby said.

"I started to feel better, and I wanted to see how you were doing," David said.

"Did you nail the clubhouse windows shut as a joke?" Bobby demanded. "Because if you did, it isn't very funny."

"David wouldn't do anything like that," Sam said.

"Of course I wouldn't," David insisted.

"Somebody nailed the windows closed and kept the door shut," Bobby said. "And tonight the clubhouse flooded."

"And you think *I* did it?" David said, astonished. "Why would I do a thing like that?"

David wouldn't do something like that, Joe thought. *But who would?*

"Maybe Damont's the guilty party," Sam said.

"I told you, he's sick with the flu," David said. He looked around at Sam and Bobby and Joe. Joe felt Sam studying him in way she never had before. He felt Bobby's eyes on him, and then David's, too. He suddenly noticed how everybody was looking at everybody else.

Joe felt unnerved. This was just like what was happening in the Agatha Christie mystery he was reading. All the remaining people stuck on the island were becoming more and more nervous. And the more upset they became, the more important it was for them to find the killer. They started to suspect one another, just like what was happening there in Jackson Park! But that didn't help anyone in the book, and Joe was sure it wasn't going to help anyone in the park.

David walked over to the clubhouse windows and touched the nails with his fingers. "This is so strange. These nails have square heads," he said, amazed. "This kind of a nail hasn't been used to construct anything since this clubhouse was built—maybe even earlier."

Sam shuddered.

Henrietta shrank back.

"Ghosts can't hammer," Joe said firmly.

Henrietta reached for Bobby's hand and started tugging him toward their bikes.

"Let's all get out of here," Bobby said.

116

Chapter Fifteen

Soaked and puzzled, Joe returned home. Wishbone ran alongside him. Now what was he going to do? He went into the house with Wishbone.

As soon as Ellen saw the two dripping forms, she was startled. "Are you all right? What happened to you?"

"It poured earlier, and the clubhouse got flooded," Joe said.

"Get out of those wet clothes before you get sick, and I'll make you some hot chocolate. And Wishbone, you let me dry you off. There's a towel in the linen closet with your name on it."

Wishbone was nearly dry, and the hot chocolate was ready when Joe came downstairs, in a clean, dry shirt and pants. He might have been warm and dry, but he still felt like shivering. He sat at the kitchen table and told Ellen about everything that had happened at the clubhouse earlier in the evening.

"It *is* strange," Ellen admitted, after Joe had filled her in on all the details. "But who would do such a thing?" she asked. Joe shrugged his shoulders miserably. Ellen patted his arm. "I'm just glad you're all right. I have some good news that might cheer you up a little," Ellen said. "Wanda called earlier and told me the parts for the truck finally came in. It's going to be fixed tomorrow. The truckers said they can have the clubhouse here by Saturday."

Joe yawned and finished the last of the hot chocolate. Beside him, Wishbone sat and wagged his tail.

Ellen studied her son. "You look exhausted. Why don't you go to bed?"

But that night, in bed, Joe couldn't sleep. He kept thinking about the mysterious events that had occurred and wondered why he couldn't solve them. Wishbone camped out at the side of his bed. He looked up at Joe, as if he were trying to offer comfort. Joe leaned over and scratched Wishbone behind his ears. Then he picked up his book, *Ten Little Indians*. He had almost finished reading it, yet he was no closer to figuring out who the killer was than any of the remaining characters in the book were!

Joe read and read. There were only two people left on the island now. He kept reading, as fast as he could, trying with each new clue to figure out who the killer

was. It had to be one or the other of the guests, but he couldn't guess which one it was. Joe had become almost obsessed with figuring out the puzzle of the murders, and he quickly turned the pages. But then, to his shock, both of the remaining characters died!

Joe looked up from his book, astonished. He leafed back through the book, thinking he must have missed a page that explained what had actually happened. This book didn't make sense! How could both of the guests die? If everyone was dead, who was the killer, then? A ghost? Joe sat up straighter in bed. Wishbone, lying on the floor beside him, lifted his head and gave Joe a curious look. "It's okay, Wishbone," Joe said.

Joe flipped to the next chapter. Maybe he would discover the solution there. That chapter was different from all the others. It was written as if it were a letter. It didn't take Joe long to figure out that the letter was a confession! It was a message in a bottle written by the judge, one of the first characters who had been killed. He wrote that, in fact, he hadn't been killed at all! He had faked his own death so no one would suspect him as the murderer. He had hidden on the island, coming out only to kill another guest each time, until there were none.

Maybe I'm just like the people in my book, looking for the wrong suspects, Joe thought. He tried to go over the clubhouse haunting in his mind. Henrietta had confessed being responsible for some of the hauntings, but she couldn't possibly have performed those earlier that night. She was right there with them. Besides, she was too frightened. Joe had thought it was Damont at first, but Damont was home sick with the flu. He hadn't been in school that day. *Sick with the flu,* Joe thought. Everyone in the book Joe was reading thought the judge was dead, but he was actually alive and hiding out to do his mischief anonymously.

Suddenly, Joe got the same excited feeling that he had right when he was about to try to score a basket in basketball. Joe got out of bed and went to the phone. He had decided to call Damont. Wishbone padded along behind Joe. The boy would call up Damont's mother and say he needed to tell Damont about a special homework assignment.

Joe dialed the phone.

"Hello?" said Mrs. Jones.

"Hi, Mrs. Jones, this is Joe Talbot," Joe said. "Sorry to call you so late. I'm in Damont's science class. I just wanted to tell him about an important assignment we got today. I know he's been out sick."

There was silence at the other end of the line. Joe's heart was pounding so hard that he was positive Mrs. Jones could hear it right through the phone. "Damont's been out sick?" she echoed. "But he's not sick. In fact, he's been out of the house all evening."

Joe felt stunned. He said a polite good-bye and then hung up quickly. He went back to his room and lay back down on his bed, his heart still pounding. Damont wasn't sick! Joe would have to trap him somehow. But how? He looked back at his book, leafing through the pages. He tried to figure out a connection between what was happening in the book and what was happening at the clubhouse. No one in *Ten Little Indians* suspected that the judge was the guilty one, because they all thought he was dead. No one suspected Damont anymore, because they all thought he had the flu. The killer in Joe's book confessed because he said he wanted some public recognition, the way all great artists did. That was just another way of saying he wanted to brag about what he had done. And that was another way of saying that the killer was just like Damont, who was always bragging to Joe or somebody else at school.

Clues, Joe thought. *Bragging.* Joe bolted up in bed. He suddenly had an idea about how to trap Damont!

As soon as school let out the next day, Joe grabbed his bike outside. Damont had missed classes again that day. Joe hadn't told any of his other friends from the club what his plan was. He wanted to be sure it would work, first. He had a lot to do before he could go over to the clubhouse. He biked as fast as he could, stopping briefly at Wanda's, then going home for a snack and to pick up Wishbone.

"I think I know how to solve the mystery, Mom," Joe told Ellen, as she poured him some milk. Then Ellen took one of the cookies that was on the plate on the table.

She grinned. "Do you want to tell me how?" she asked.

Joe shook his head excitedly. "I'll tell you when it's solved," he promised.

Joe quickly finished his snack. Then he gave Wishbone one of his favorite ginger snaps. Wishbone's whole body wagged with delight. He polished off the treat in seconds.

"Okay, let's go," Joe told Wishbone. "It's mystery-solving time." The two pals left the house in a flash. Wishbone trotted eagerly alongside Joe's bike. He usually knew what Joe was up to, but this time he didn't have a clue. He bet that it was something exciting, something a dog would love to get his paws into.

They were passing by Wanda's house when her front door opened and out scooted Pixie the cat. Wishbone sniffed. "Uh-oh, I smell trouble," he said.

Pixie was following him.

Joe turned around. "Hey, we've got company, Wishbone," he said.

"*Uninvited* company," Wishbone said.

With Pixie following Wishbone and Joe at her slow pace, the ride to the clubhouse seemed extra long. They were halfway there when an elderly couple passed them going the other way and did a double-take. "Isn't that adorable!" the woman exclaimed, clapping her hands. "A kitty and a doggie!"

"Don't call me 'doggie'!" Wishbone scolded. "And we *aren't* a couple!"

The woman bent down and petted Pixie first, then Wishbone. The terrier cringed a little.

The situation got even worse two blocks farther away when they passed by a man carrying a bag of groceries. "And what do we have here?" He laughed. He nodded at Wishbone. "I commend you for your choice of friends."

"Pixie's *not* my friend!" Wishbone cried.

The man bent down and petted Pixie, who purred. Then it was Wishbone's turn to be petted. Finally, the man continued on his way.

Joe biked as fast as he could for the remaining distance to the clubhouse. Wishbone put his paws into high gear, too, and by the time they got to the clubhouse, he was panting. He stopped to look around. Pixie was gone.

"Come on, Wishbone," Joe said, getting off his bike and parking it quickly. His sneakers squished as he made his way across the soggy ground. The flood yesterday had turned the ground more into mud than grass. Wishbone thought about rolling in the mud, but his attention quickly turned to Joe, who reached for something in his knapsack.

Wishbone couldn't help but be curious about what the contents was. He sniffed, trying to figure out what the mystery item was. It was wrapped in a blue towel. Wishbone sniffed harder. "Oh, I know that scent!" he said. "Tuna! Yarn! Trouble! It's—it's Pixie!" He turned and there was Pixie, tripping through the wet grass toward him.

Joe laughed. He opened the door to the clubhouse. Although there wasn't a trace of water inside anymore, the place still smelled damp. When Joe walked inside and stepped on the wood floor, it seemed to give a little under his feet. The other kids were already sitting around the card table, smoothing out the playing cards, which had curled up from being soaked by the water.

"Hi, everyone," Joe said.

The kids looked up.

"Hey, look at Pixie with Wishbone!" Henrietta called.

Sam bent down and stroked Pixie. Then Wishbone scooted over and pushed his head under Sam's hand, so she had to pet him, too.

Joe suddenly pulled something out of the towel. It was a clear glass bottle filled with rose-colored liquid. "Joy de Wanda," he announced. "She loaned me some."

"Perfume?" Bobby asked.

Wishbone sneezed, and then he put a paw over his nose.

Joe shook his head excitedly. "Listen, when Wishbone and I were tailing Damont, Ms. Gilmore was wearing this perfume, and he sneezed like crazy. He was allergic to it."

Bobby looked doubtful. "But so what? I thought we proved Damont wasn't our ghost. And anyway, he's sick with the flu now."

Joe shook his head. "Not according to his mother. He's playing hooky."

"Wait a minute!" Bobby said. "So Damont could have tacked up that note, too?"

Wishbone ran over to Henrietta and began to lick her hand encouragingly. He knew that a dog's friendly licking did a lot to give a person confidence.

Henrietta petted his head and then drew herself up. "I . . . wrote . . . that . . . note," she said slowly.

Bobby looked shocked. Sam shook her head in amazement. David looked stunned.

"I didn't nail the windows shut," Henrietta added quickly. "And I'm sorry for what I did do." She suddenly relaxed. "And I'm glad I told all of you. It's no fun keeping secrets."

"Good girl!" Wishbone said, and he gave her another lick for good measure.

Bobby was just about to speak when Pixie suddenly jumped up toward Joe. She startled him so much that he dropped the bottle of perfume. The perfume spilled out in a gush, dousing Pixie. Then the bottle smashed on the floor. "Oh, no!" Joe cried. "I was going to dribble it like a trail!"

Pixie's fur was soaked. Wishbone drew back.

Joe bent down, wrinkling his nose. He gently prodded Pixie to go outside. Then he shut the door. "Shut it tight," Wishbone said.

Suddenly something began to thump against the side of the clubhouse.

An object sailed in through the window that Joe had broken the night before. It whizzed past Sam.

"I'll fetch!" Wishbone cried, leaping up and trying to snatch it in his jaw. "Ouch! That hurts my teeth!" he said, dropping it, so it rolled on the floor.

"It's a pinecone!" Joe said. There was a sudden loud moaning outside.

David ran to the door to open it. But it wouldn't budge, even when he tugged on it. He banged against the wood with his hands. Suddenly, the moaning stopped. But then there was another sound. Louder. Clearer. *Sneezing.* Lots and lots of sneezing!

Joe grinned from ear to ear. "Ghosts don't sneeze!" he cried. "But guess who does?"

Joe grabbed for the door, which suddenly flew open. Everybody ran outside. There, racing into the woods, sneezing, was Damont!

"Hold it right there!" Wishbone called out.

"Damont!" Sam shouted.

Damont suddenly stumbled. He tripped and fell to the ground. The pinecones spilled all around him.

Then he sat up, defeated, his hands cupping his face, as he sneezed and sneezed.

Everyone rushed toward him, crowding around him in a circle.

"Why did you do it, Damont?" Joe asked.

Damont shrugged. "That clubhouse should have been mine," he insisted. "I bought fifty tickets. The odds were in my favor. You each bought only one ticket. Is that fair?" Damont sneezed again. "Get that cat away from me!" he said, shooing Pixie with his hands.

Damont stood up, shaking his head. He started to walk away. Then he suddenly turned back to face the kids.

"You'll have to admit, I was pretty clever," he said. "Did you see those nails in the windows? Antiques. My dad had them in the garage. They were my grand-father's." Damont displayed a wide grin. "I was *really* clever," he said proudly.

"Not so clever that you were able to avoid getting caught," Sam said.

The gang all watched Damont leave the park.

"We're finally safe," Sam said.

"And you were the one who figured out the mystery!" David congratulated Joe.

"I guess I did," Joe said happily. He bent down and plucked Pixie up. "Of course, I had a little help from my friends," he said, "and from a really great book." He turned to look back at the clubhouse. "Come on, it's time to get home.

Chapter Sixteen

The clubhouse seemed especially cozy to Joe that evening, after dinner. He sat at the card table watching Henrietta brush Wishbone. Pixie sat in a corner, grooming herself. The clubhouse reeked of Wanda's perfume, but Joe didn't care. He was so happy that the mystery was solved, he didn't mind at all.

Just then a bolt of lightning shot down from the sky. Thunder boomed so loudly that it made Wishbone jump. The brush Henrietta was using on his soft fur clattered to the floor.

"Uh-oh, I hope the clubhouse doesn't flood again," Sam said. She looked out at the threatening sky. "Maybe we should take off and go home."

"I have a bad feeling about this," David said.

"The weather report said there would be clear skies," Joe said.

Bobby looked out the window and shook his head. "There hasn't been a clear patch of sky to look at all day," Bobby said. "When you can't even see a single star, you know the weather is up to no good."

Suddenly, the rain began, rat-tat-tatting against the roof and the pine walls of the clubhouse. Wishbone barked and headed for the door.

"Here we go again," Joe said.

A brilliant bolt of lightning forked through the sky. The sky suddenly flashed gold, and there was a loud, thunderous sound. Sam jumped. The lightning had come so close that the very air around them seemed to be burning.

It hurt Joe's nose and made his eyes water. There was a deep sizzling smell that made Joe's stomach clench. Suddenly the air grew still again. The night seemed absolutely quiet. Then, all at once, the sky opened up. Thunder *boomed.* It was so loud that Joe and Sam clapped their hands to their ears.

Bobby, though, looked fascinated. He moved closer to the window and stared up at the sky in pure amazement. "It's a natural wonder," he said.

Henrietta tried to tug him away, but he shook himself free. A huge, bright zigzag of lightning crashed down again. The force of the lightning seemed to make the clubhouse shake. Henrietta jumped up. "That was close! We'd better get out of here fast!" she exclaimed.

Everyone began to gather up their things. Henrietta grabbed the brush. Sam collected the cards. Joe scooped up Wishbone. They raced out the front door. Pixie ran ahead of them. Rain slashed their faces. The air seemed hot, as if any moment it might explode into flames. Suddenly, a bolt of lightning shot across the sky and struck a tree right by the clubhouse! The tree made a loud *crack* and began to fall.

"Look out!" Joe shouted. "Get out of the way!"

Horrified, he grabbed Sam and pushed her out of the way of the doomed tree. Bobby tugged Henrietta toward him. David ran toward the woods. The tree continued to fall. "Oh, no!" Joe cried. For a moment, it looked to him as though the tree were moving in slow motion. It seemed to sway in the air, almost as if it were dancing. The leaves fluttered back and forth.

Then, suddenly, the motion of the tree speeded up. It moved so fast Joe couldn't tell which way it was falling. Finally, the tree fell right on the clubhouse, smashing it into pieces on the ground with a loud, horrifying crash! Boards broke and splintered and flew all over the ground. Glass shattered with the sound of a thousand bells all ringing at once.

Joe stood in the pouring rain, watching in horror. "Oh, no!" he cried. "This can't be happening!"

The clubhouse didn't look like a clubhouse any-more. It had become a bunch of scrap lumber piled into a heap. It was impossible to tell that only minutes ago the wood had actually been a building.

Joe was soaking wet, but he couldn't tear himself away from the scene. Wishbone tugged frantically at his pal's pants leg, trying to urge him forward. Sam and David each grabbed one of Joe's arms and pulled him away.

Joe stumbled forward. He felt as if he were awakening from a nightmare. He had spent so much time solving the mystery of who was haunting the clubhouse. Everything was supposed to have ended wonderfully—and now this storm had come out of nowhere. His clubhouse was destroyed. It hadn't been ruined by a ghost, either. This was a force of nature. He dimly heard Wishbone barking. He felt Sam pulling at his arm, urging him to leave.

"Joe!" David called, pulling at his other arm.

Another blast of thunder made a loud, echoing *boom*. More forks of jagged lightning zigzagged across the sky, in a brilliant display of light. The noise was so loud that Henrietta clapped her hands over her ears. The lightning was so close that Henrietta began to cry.

"Let's go, let's go!" she cried.

Joe took one last look at what had been his treasured clubhouse. Then, reluctantly, Joe let himself be led away.

Chapter Seventeen

By the time Joe and Wishbone got to the front of their house, they were soaked to the skin. Joe was so miserable that all he could think about was getting into dry clothes and having something hot to drink.

"Joe!" Ellen said, coming out the front door. She was in her yellow raincoat and carrying an umbrella. "I was just about to go to try to find you," she said. "I got really worried when the storm blew up and I saw the lightning. Please tell me coming home sopping wet isn't going to become a habit!" Ellen ushered both him and Wishbone inside. "You go get dry. You can tell me later what happened *this* time!"

Joe went upstairs and toweled off and changed his clothes. Ellen rubbed Wishbone dry downstairs. In a while, Joe joined Ellen and Wishbone in the kitchen. Miserably, he told his mother about the evening's events as they sat at the table.

"Thank goodness everyone is all right," Ellen said. Joe could see the mix of worry and relief on her face.

"I'm so sorry about your clubhouse," Ellen said. "Maybe it can be repaired," she suggested.

Joe shook his head. "It was too destroyed, Mom," he said. "The tree just smashed it to pieces."

Wishbone jumped up into Joe's lap, nuzzling him with his cool, damp nose.

"Thanks, Wishbone." Joe looked at his mother. "At least I had the clubhouse for a while."

"I'm glad you had it for as long as you did, Joe," Ellen said.

Just then, the phone rang. Ellen got up to answer it. She nodded as the voice at the other end spoke.

"Yes," she said into the receiver. "I understand. . . ." She looked at Joe. "It's the truck driver," she mouthed. "No," she said. "Lightning hit it. There is no clubhouse. . . . All right, then."

Ellen hung up the phone.

"Imagine that," she said. "The trucker wanted to confirm the delivery of the clubhouse for tomorrow. Now he and his workers are just going to cart away the debris," she said. She came over and hugged Joe. "I'm very sorry about your clubhouse, Joe," she said.

"Me, too," Joe answered sadly.

Joe slept in late Saturday morning. He awoke to a ringing phone—it was David.

"Joe, guess what happened. Damont was grounded!" David said.

"For skipping school?" Joe asked.

"Yes," David responded.

"Well, I'm not surprised," Joe said. Then he chuckled. "After what he put us through, Damont deserves to spend a week all by himself in the haunted Murphy house!"

After hanging up the phone, Joe looked down at Wishbone and laughed. Joe was almost certain that Wishbone was actually *smiling.*

Joe tried not to think about the clubhouse, but something kept pulling him to Jackson Park. Later that afternoon, he headed for Jackson Park on his bike. Wishbone stayed close by his side. He wasn't sure why, but he felt as if he had to see the spot where the clubhouse had been just one more time.

When Joe and Wishbone got near the clearing, he could see that all the wood from the clubhouse was gone. Joe stood right in the center of the clearing, exactly where the clubhouse had been.

"Ms. Gilmore was right, Wishbone," Joe said. "This is really a pretty spot." He looked around. "Boy, I actually thought there might have been a ghost," he said. "But it was only a little girl afraid of being left out—and Damont."

He began to feel a little better. He had overcome his fear about ghosts once and for all. And natural forces, not ghosts, had destroyed the clubhouse. Joe thought about his father trying to solve the imaginary mysteries in his books. Solving real mysteries was hard work. Joe wished his father was still around so he could tell him about the one he had just been involved with.

Wishbone suddenly wagged his tail so hard that it looked as if he were shaking his entire body.

Joe looked down at the ground. Immediately, he

froze in place. There, right between his sneakers, popping straight up, was a single white wildflower! It was just like the kind of flower that Amanda, the Oakdale ghost, had loved. A chill raced through Joe. "Did you see that wildflower there before?" he said to Wishbone. Joe was sure it wasn't there a minute ago.

He stepped back, away from the flower. Wishbone whined deep in his throat. He also backed up.

Suddenly, Joe felt as if someone was standing there watching him. He started to shiver uncontrollably. "Let's get out of here, Wishbone," he said.

Joe couldn't ride home fast enough. He flung his bike down on the front lawn and ran into the house, Wishbone at his heels.

"Mom!" he called. He raced into the kitchen,

where Ellen was sitting at the table, drinking a cup of tea. Wishbone trotted in and sat down near Ellen.

"Joe, you look as if you've seen a ghost," Ellen said.

"Maybe I *have*," Joe said. "We got to the spot where the clubhouse was, and it was all clean, like nothing had ever been there before."

"Well, you knew the truck was going to come to take away the debris," Ellen said.

Joe shook his head. "You don't understand. There was *nothing* there—and then, suddenly, there was *something* there. There was a single white wildflower, growing up in the middle of nothing. It had never been there before. And there were no other flowers around. Ms. Gilmore showed me and the other kids this book about ghosts the other day. It said there was a ghost of Oakdale—a little girl who used to go into the woods to pick white wildflowers." Joe stopped talking abruptly. "What does it mean, Mom?" he asked urgently. "I thought there was no such thing as ghosts! I worked really hard to convince myself that there weren't, that it was just superstition."

Ellen studied Joe. "Well, what do *you* think it means, Joe?" Ellen said gently.

"I don't know. I keep trying to think what Dad would make of it. I wonder how he would have solved this mystery."

Ellen smiled at Joe. "Joe," she said, "sometimes I look at you and I see a lot of your father in you. And that's wonderful. But I don't want you to *be* your father. I want you to be you. What's important is how *you* would solve this mystery," Ellen said.

"There's got to be an explanation," Joe said, "like

in the Agatha Christie book. For a while, it seemed as if there was no solution, but there was. The killer wrote a letter, a message in a bottle. All the loose bits and pieces were tied up at the end of the story. It was a surprise ending, but still, everything was solved."

"But Joe," Ellen said softly, "that's not always the case in real-life situations. Sometimes there aren't always nice, neat explanations for everything. But that's the beauty of life."

"What do you mean?" Joe asked.

"I mean that maybe things aren't always so clear-cut and definite. Maybe the truth about some things is a little bit more hazy—not so easy to put your finger on. Not everything can be proven. We don't have all the answers to everything. A little mystery makes life a lot more interesting."

"Do you think there's a ghost?" Joe asked.

"I don't know," Ellen said. "But what's important is, do you?"

"I guess I don't know, either," Joe said. "I just know that something I can't explain happened—something incredible."

"And doesn't that make life more interesting—not having all the answers?" Ellen asked.

Wishbone barked, wagging his tail, as if to say he agreed with Ellen.

Ellen reached over and ruffled Joe's hair.

"I guess you're right," Joe said. "Still, it's so . . . I don't know—weird."

Wishbone looked toward the door.

"I think I'll take Wishbone for a walk," Joe said.

Wishbone wagged his tail even harder, almost as

if he had been trying to tell Joe that was exactly what he wanted.

Wishbone frisked in the cool, clean air. He was happy to be outside taking a walk with his best friend. "So, we don't have the clubhouse, Joe," he said. "But we do have each other, and that's what matters the most."

They were walking down their block. Joe was tossing a ball in the air and catching it. Wishbone felt it in his bones that they were going to play catch in the park. Suddenly, though, Wishbone became aware of a familiar scent.

"It's Pixie," he said. "Maybe we should switch gears and head in the opposite direction."

He looked over toward Wanda's house. Wanda was standing on her porch, holding Pixie and petting her. There was another woman with her on the porch, too. Wishbone didn't recognize her. She was tall and dressed in a blue suit. She had a bright crown of blond hair. This other woman was reaching her hand out to pet Pixie, too.

"Two cat lovers," Wishbone said. "That's not a good sign."

"Hi, Joe," Wanda called out. "My ad in the *Chronicle* worked. Pixie's real owner called. She's been out looking for Pixie for days. Come and say hello."

Wishbone's ears perked up. "Did she say Pixie's real owner? Does that mean what I think it does? This is one disappearing act I'd pay to see."

"Hi, Wishbone," Wanda said, as Joe and Wishbone approached the porch steps. "This is Mrs. Merton."

"You don't know how worried I've been," Mrs. Merton said. "I had this pretty kitty in the car with me, and she just leaped out the window and got lost. It was so terrible. I called everyone I knew. I advertised. I even offered a reward. She's very valuable."

"She is?" said Joe.

"Why, yes. Her mother was a show cat," said Mrs. Merton. "When she's older, she'll be one, too."

"A show cat?" Joe asked, confused.

Mrs. Merton nodded. "Her mother won Best of Show three times in a row. Pixie's a pedigree."

"That kitten is a pedigree?" Wishbone said. "Things are getting stranger and stranger around here all the time."

Wanda sighed. "I sure hate to give her up. What did you say her real name was again?"

"Queen Maiden the First," Mrs. Merton said with a smile.

"A queen? She's royalty?" Wishbone said.

"I'll tell you what," Mrs. Merton said to Wanda. "Maybe if Queen Maiden ever has kittens, you'd like one—for free, of course, as a reward."

"Say no, Wanda," Wishbone begged.

"I'd be thrilled to have such a beautiful pet!" Wanda said enthusiastically.

Pixie leaped from Wanda's arms and snuggled up to Wishbone. Wishbone couldn't help himself. "Okay, quick good-byes are the best," Wishbone said, "especially when it comes to cats."

Mrs. Merton scooped the kitten up in her arms a moment later.

"Boy," Joe said. "So all the Oakdale mysteries are solved now. We know where Pixie came from—and where she's going. We know who was haunting the clubhouse."

"But we don't know what our next adventure is going to be, and that's part of the fun," Wishbone said. He thought about Pixie, and how that was a mystery he could never solve: Why did people like cats!?

Joe tossed his ball up in the air again. "It was nice meeting you," Joe said to Pixie's owner. He nodded to Wanda and then looked at Wishbone. "Come on, Wishbone, let's go to the park and celebrate with a game of fetch."

Does this boy know me, or what? Wishbone thought. He trotted happily beside Joe. Joe threw the ball up in the air and caught it, again and again. Joe suddenly stopped and bent down and scratched Wishbone right where he liked it the most, behind his ears. "What I like is no mystery to you, Joe," Wishbone said. "And until the next *real* mystery comes along, toss me that ball!"

About Caroline Leavitt

Caroline Leavitt loves mysteries almost as much as she loves that dog Wishbone! Writing a WISHBONE mystery was really a thrill for her.

An award-winning author, Caroline has written six novels, including two other WISHBONE titles: *Robinhound Crusoe,* based on Daniel Defoe's *Robinson Crusoe;* and *The Prince and the Pooch,* based on Mark Twain's *The Prince and the Pauper.* Although her other novels are written for adults, she enjoys writing for children. She has also written magazine articles, and screenplays for the movies.

Caroline wishes she had had a clubhouse when she was a child. What she has now is a 124-year-old house that she shares with her husband, Jeff; toddler son, Max; and tortoise, Minnie. In the future, Caroline plans to share the house with a puppy, too, when her son is old enough to take care of it. She hopes the puppy will be as smart and cute as that talkative dog Wishbone!

Now Playing on Your VCR...

Two exciting **WISHBONE** stories on video!

Ready for an adventure? Then leap right in with **Wishbone**™ as he takes you on a thrilling journey through two great action-packed stories. First, there are haunted houses, buried treasure, and mysterious graves in two back-to-back episodes of *A Tail in Twain*, starring **Wishbone** as Tom Sawyer. Then, no one is more powerful than Hercules...or rather **Wishbone**, in *Hercules*   *Unleashed*, featuring exciting new footage!   It's more fun than a flea dip! It's **Wishbone** on home video.

WiSHBONE™

Available wherever videos are sold.